THE WITCH'S
EYE

THE WITCH'S EYE

Phyllis Reynolds Naylor

ILLUSTRATED BY

Joe Burleson

Delacorte Press

Published by
Delacorte Press
Bantam Doubleday Dell Publishing Group, Inc.
666 Fifth Avenue
New York, New York 10103

Library of Congress Cataloging in Publication Data

Naylor, Phyllis Reynolds.
    The witch's eye / by Phyllis Reynolds Naylor ; illustrated by Joe Burleson.
        p.   cm.
    Summary: Though suspected witch-neighbor Mrs. Tuggle has died, her glass eye resurfaces, bringing new dangers and terrors to Lynn's family.
    ISBN 0-385-30157-X
    [1. Witchcraft—Fiction.]   I. Burleson, Joe, ill.   II. Title.
PZ7.N24Wle   1990
[Fic]—dc20   89-77237
                                                                CIP
                                                                AC

Manufactured in the United States of America

October 1990

10 9 8 7 6 5 4 3 2 1
BVG

To everyone who liked the first three

THE WITCH'S

EYE

chapter one

It's over.

In one corner of her bed, Lynn huddled against the wall, a quilt over her shoulders. Despite the quilt, she shivered.

"It's over," she said, this time aloud, as though saying it made it true. As though all she had to do was speak the words, and everything that had happened would blow away and leave no trace, like blowing dust off the top of the dresser.

During the day she and Marjorie Beasley—whom everyone except grown-ups called "Mouse"—went to school, took piano lessons, or swam at the Y. On weekends they helped Lynn's older sister make jam out of winter pears, something Judith had just learned to do. During the day they kept busy.

It was at night, when the house was still, that the thoughts came back, the thoughts that brought on shivers. The worst part was that Lynn's father tried to make it seem as though what Lynn remembered hadn't happened—not in the way she thought. Sometimes, Dad said, when you are very frightened or upset, you see and hear things not quite like they really are, imagination all mixed up with truth, and then it's hard to sort out.

"We did, you know," Mouse said when Lynn told her that one day at recess.

"Did what?"

"See what we saw and hear what we heard."

"I know," said Lynn, and they went on twisting slowly around and around on the swings, making patterns in the dirt with the sides of their sneakers.

Marjorie, with her straight dark hair and huge glasses, looked more like an owl than a mouse. Lynn, on the other hand, had a longer, more angular face—gray eyes and faint freckles on pale skin, her hair pulled back in a ponytail. Everyone said she resembled her father, but their ideas were poles apart.

"You can come to me with anything, Lynn," Father had told her only a few days before, "but keep it to facts this time, okay? Try, *really* try, to separate facts from worries. It will be better for you."

For Mother, he meant. He was worried about Mother. All those weeks she had been working on her book in an upstairs room at Mrs. Tuggle's, Mother had been behaving strangely, as though she were under the old woman's spell. Now that Mrs. Tuggle's house had burned to the ground, and the old woman along with it, Mother was gradually improving, but she still stared out the window a lot and took long walks by herself. The family hoped that, in time, Mrs. Tuggle's influence over her would disappear entirely, but meanwhile, they were taking no chances. It was understood, if not said, that *it was over* as far as talking about it with Mother went.

At the dinner table, if the conversation drifted even slightly toward the events of the last year, Father always had a funny story to tell, something that had happened at work, something he hoped would make Mother laugh. Lynn watched the way he would tell his little story and look at Mother sideways to see if she was smiling. Sometimes she was. Sometimes not.

And so, Lynn sat in the corner of her bed with a tablet on her lap, a stub of a pencil, and decided that she would write it down, as clearly as she could remember, everything exactly as it had happened, no exaggeration. So that if she should ever *need* to remember . . . She shivered again.

It all started a year ago with Judith, she wrote on the tablet, pushing back strands of light brown hair that fell over her eyes. *When Judith wanted to learn to sew last spring, Mrs. Tuggle offered to teach her. Judith began taking her dress patterns and walking up the hill to Mrs. Tuggle's house once or twice a week in the evenings, and nobody suspected a thing —except me.*

Lynn rested her back against the wall. At first not even she knew it was witchcraft. Hadn't even suspected. Her sister seemed to be changing in front of their very eyes, yet Mother said it was because Judith was growing up, and girls that age were moody.

And then one day Lynn had seen her down at the creek, kneeling on the bank and crooning, her hands cupped in the water. And as Lynn crept forward, staring, she saw that tadpoles swam right into Judith's hands. Judith picked them up and put them in a jar that she kept in her bedroom. When Lynn tried it, however, the tadpoles swam away from her fingers. It was spooky.

This was followed by the night Mr. and Mrs. Morley, Lynn's parents, went out of town to a conference, and Mother had asked Mrs. Tuggle to stay in the house overnight. Lynn and Mouse, meanwhile, had picked up a rare book about witchcraft from Mr. Beasley's bookstore, and had read that witches grease their broomsticks with the fat of little children. To give a child to witches, they had read, you must leave him outside at midnight so when the witches ride by they can carry him off. And that night, the night Mrs. Tuggle stayed, when Lynn awoke about midnight to hear Judith trying to coax their five-year-old brother outside, she had screamed and carried on so hysterically that she had stopped whatever Judith and Mrs. Tuggle were up to. Judith had said she just wanted to show Stevie the meteor shower. But after that, she got very sick, and when she recovered, she stopped going to Mrs. Tuggle's.

Lynn stopped writing and let out her breath. She and Mouse had thought this was the end of it. And it *did* seem to be the end of it for Judith. She got well and didn't act strange anymore, but it was about then that Lynn and Mouse noticed the crows —nine of them, following the two girls wherever they went. Flying from tree to tree as they walked to school; sitting on a branch outside, their beady eyes fixed on the classroom window; in the trees at night, waiting, watching. And then that terrifying night when Mr. Beasley was away, Lynn had stayed over with Mouse, and suddenly the house was surrounded by cats and crows, clawing and scratching. The girls had not just imagined it, either. The lead crow was trying to come down the chimney when Mouse closed the fireplace flue just in time; the huge bird had been killed as the flue flap clamped down on him. His body was still there when Mr. Beasley came home the next day.

Lynn put her pencil down once again and rubbed her fingers, one at a time. She was getting to the part that was hardest to think about. The part where Mother, who wrote children's books, decided to rent one of the upstairs rooms in Mrs. Tuggle's house, for a studio. The more she wrote at Mrs. Tuggle's, the more irritable and impulsive she became. And then Mrs. Tuggle's house was struck by lightning, and Lynn was able to rescue her mother only by tearing off the charm that Mrs. Tuggle's cat used to wear, a gift to Mother from the old woman. It was then that the power lifted, and Mother was able to get up out of her chair and crawl out the window just in time, as the house was engulfed in flames.

"It's over now," Father had said when he arrived at the scene, and hugged Mother.

"It's over, Stevie," he told Lynn's little brother when the small boy cried in all the confusion. "We're a family again. It's over. Mrs. Tuggle was a very mixed-up woman who may have had a guilty conscience, but her house is gone, she's gone, and that's all there is to it."

But not quite.

Because the next day, when Lynn and Mouse had gone up the hill to stare at the ashes, Lynn had seen something in the rubble—something smooth and shiny and green. And when she bent over to look, she saw that it was an eye, a glass eye: Mrs. Tuggle's green glass eye, which had never quite matched her gray one. Lynn had backed away, but as she turned one last time, she thought that the eye winked at her. Fact or feeling? Had the eye actually winked, or was she only *afraid* that it had?

In any case, when she went back up the hill a week later, the bulldozers were there clearing the land, and the glass eye was gone.

So what was the problem now? Mother was beginning to come out of whatever trancelike state she had been in; Judith, who seemed to have forgotten her own months with Mrs. Tuggle, had taken over some of the cooking; the TV came on after dinner, and Lynn and Judith and Stevie sat on the couch together watching *The Cosby Show*. Father spread his lawyer's briefs out on the dining room table, as always, to go over his work for the next day. Just like always. So what *was* wrong?

Lynn wrote that last sentence on her tablet and ended it with a dark, heavy question mark. She didn't know the answer. A feeling, that was all, the kind of thing her father didn't want her to talk about anymore.

"If you actually see something, Lynn, or hear something that bothers you, I want to know about it, of course. But don't upset the family with things you just *feel* might have happened, or that you only *think* are going to happen. Anything is possible, but only a small percent is probable. There's a difference."

It even seemed to Lynn as though there were times that Mouse was ready to forget. *Wanted* to forget. She was already talking about going to visit her mother that summer, and when your parents split up, as Marjorie's had done, leaving Mouse with her father and the Beasley book shop, going to see your mother must be a big occasion. So mostly Lynn kept her thoughts to herself. She had seen nothing suspicious. Heard nothing suspicious. All she had was The Feeling, and she didn't know what she could say about that.

She stopped writing at last and let go of the pencil, opening and closing her fingers to get rid of the cramp. There was something about getting it all down on paper that helped—getting it down in words made it definite and sure, so that no matter how many people told her that *It* hadn't happened —the witchcraft—she would know better.

Lynn actually began to feel hungry. All she'd eaten for dinner was a tiny piece of chicken and a bite of mashed potato. She hadn't even touched her dessert.

That's what she thought about now. Dessert. Two Oreo cookies, maybe, with a glass of milk.

Keeping the quilt around her shoulders and holding the ends up so she wouldn't trip, Lynn made her way across the floor. On the other side of the heavy curtain that divided their huge third-floor bedroom,

Judith slept soundly. Lynn could hear the little noises Judith made when she breathed through her mouth.

She started down the stairs to the second floor where Stevie slept in the small bedroom across from Father and Mother. There was a night light in the hall outside the bathroom to help people find their way in the dark. Lynn looked at her own shadow as she passed, the quilt over her shoulders making her look like an old humpbacked woman. The shiver again.

Some of her friends had grandmothers who were old and stooped and wrinkled and wonderful. What had made Mrs. Tuggle so different? At what point had she become a witch? And then Lynn realized she was thinking the *W* word again, the word her father didn't want to hear anymore. As though merely talking about it made it happen. So who was superstitious now—Lynn or her dad?

Down in the kitchen, Lynn turned on the light and found the cookies. She poured herself a glass of milk and squeezed her quilt-covered self into a seat at the table, where she separated each cookie, scraped the thick creamy-white filling off with her teeth, and held it in her mouth while the sweetness dissolved on her tongue and ran down her throat. When the filling was gone, she took one of the four chocolate cookie halves that were left and dunked it in the milk, eating that next.

It was strange being down in the kitchen at three-fifteen in the morning. The house was so still. Not even the furnace was on, making its low, rushing sound. The refrigerator was quiet too. When Lynn stopped chewing, in fact, so that not even the noise of her teeth disturbed her, she heard no sound at all —not even the tick of a clock. The sound of silence.

And then, just as she picked up the second piece of cookie, she heard someone whisper. She paused, her mouth half open. She waited for about ten seconds before she swallowed. *Imagination.* That's what her dad would say. "Lynn, my imaginative daughter," he called her sometimes. Fact or fancy? Had she heard anything or not?

The whisper came again.

"What?" Lynn said, jerking around, expecting to see someone standing behind her, but no one was there. Goose bumps rose on her arms as the words of the whisper became more distinct:

> "From the shadows of the pool,
> Black as midnight, thick as gruel,
> Come, my nymphs, and you shall be
> Silent images of me."

Lynn put down the cookie and stood up. That was the song Mrs. Tuggle had taught Judith, the song the old woman had sung to them the time she came to take care of them overnight, when the lights went out in the storm.

> "Suck the honey from my lips,
> Dance upon my fingertips.
> When the darkness tolls the hour,
> I shall have you in my power."

Not even bothering to turn out the light, Lynn clutched at the quilt and headed for the stairs. The whisper followed after her, growing louder, in fact, as she reached the second floor:

> "Fast upon us, spirits all,
>   Listen for our whispered call.
>   Whistling kettle, tinkling bell,
>   Weave your web and spin your spell."

On the third floor at last, Lynn rushed across the rug, flung herself into bed, and lay there, her eyes tightly shut, her body shaking. The whisper had stopped, and the house was still once again.

chapter two

"So who left the light on in the kitchen last night, and crumbs all over the table?"

It was Mother making breakfast this morning, Mother looking better than she had for a long time as she turned pancakes there at the stove, her long honey-blond hair pulled back and tied with a scarf. She was actually smiling, as though the crumbs didn't really matter.

"I did," Lynn said, taking her place at the table quickly and drinking her orange juice. "I'm sorry."

"I thought I was the last one to go to bed, Lynn," her father said. "What time were you in the kitchen?"

Lynn felt her father's eyes on her as she poured syrup on her pancakes. She didn't look up. "Oh, I don't know. I got hungry sometime in the night."

Mr. Morley returned to his newspaper. "Stocks are down," he murmured, turning the page. "Maybe it's time to buy some shares of IBM."

"Maybe," said Mother.

This was what made it so awful: The rest of the family went on like always, because no one else had heard the singing. Little Stevie was fussing because Mother had put blueberries in the pancakes,

Judith was trying to study for an algebra test while she ate. . . .

I wonder if this is what it's like to be mentally ill, Lynn wondered. She wanted to be a psychiatrist when she grew up, so she was always interested in what she, and everyone else, was thinking and feeling. *If I were mentally ill,* she told herself, *I might hear voices that no one else hears. But if I were sick that way, would I be worried that I was sick? I don't know.*

Deep down, however, she knew she was *not* mentally ill. She got along well with her teachers and friends, she did not feel sad without reason, she did not believe she was a special person tuned in to a planet from outer space. Nor did she go around listening for voices, for whispers. Lynn would be wildly happy if Mrs. Tuggle was indeed gone forever and she could concentrate on something like playing Monopoly with Mouse, or making Indian bead bracelets, or just riding around town on her bike. But she knew what she had heard.

If she told her father, however, he would say, "Now, *think,* Lynn. If the whispers got louder right outside our bedroom door last night, why wouldn't we have heard them too? You know your mother's a light sleeper."

Nonetheless, Lynn felt that her father half believed her—and all that had happened. Believed but didn't want to.

During a flood last spring, when the river rose and covered the cemetery, and some of the coffins were washed out of their graves, the casket that supposedly held the remains of Mrs. Tuggle's young brother—drowned, she had said, when he was sixteen—was found not to hold a young boy at all but a woman. And the dental records showed that her name was Bertha Voight, who had once, long ago, accused Mrs. Tuggle of witchcraft, then mysteriously disappeared. Before the courts could reopen the case, however, the fire killed Mrs. Tuggle and burned her house to the ground.

It was this unsettled business, if anything, that bothered Lynn's father, because these were *facts*. It was a fact that even though Mrs. Tuggle claimed her young brother had drowned, no death certificate had ever been filed in the courthouse. The body in his grave turned out to be that of Bertha Voight. This was also a fact. Facts that Mr. Morley, being a lawyer, could handle. So as far as Lynn's father was concerned, Lynn sometimes felt, the matter was closed. No one would ever know the truth about what had really happened, since it happened long ago, and Mrs. Tuggle was dead.

Lynn could not talk to her mother about the whispers—*would* not—because it had taken all this time for Mother to recover from whatever hold Mrs. Tuggle had had on her. Lynn would not tell Judith, either, because Judith, just last summer, had also been under the old woman's spell. To remind Judith of things past might start things going again. That left only Stevie, who was too young to understand and would believe whatever Lynn told him. So the family was out. And this was what bothered Lynn—that she could not confide in the people closest to her.

She finished her pancakes, went upstairs to brush her teeth, and then went out on the sidewalk to wait for Mouse, who was already coming up the hill, dressed in her usual poncho, her arms tucked inside for warmth.

"I'm going to visit Mom this summer!" Mouse said the moment she got to Lynn. "She called last night and said we could spend a whole week together."

Lynn tried to think of what to say. She had thought Mouse was going for the whole summer. *Weeks,* anyway. When a mother leaves a family and goes off to Ohio to live, wouldn't you think she could ask her daughter to come for a month at least? Why, in fact, hadn't she taken Mouse with her?

"That's wonderful!" is what Lynn actually said. "You'll have a great time, Mouse."

They walked a half block in silence, and then Mouse herself said it: "I *was* hoping she'd invite me to stay longer."

"Maybe she just doesn't have a nice enough place for you yet."

"I'd sleep anywhere. Even the floor." Was that a tremor in Marjorie's voice?

"I know," Lynn said. The only way to make Mouse forget her mother entirely, for a time anyway, was to get her mind on something big. And so Lynn told her about the whispers.

Mouse stopped dead still on the sidewalk, her

mouth slightly open. Her eyes, behind her large, round-rimmed glasses, were huge.

"Lynn," she said hoarsely, "are you sure?"

"Positive." Lynn walked on determinedly, and Mouse gave a little skip to catch up. "Only a week ago I was trying to remember that song that Judith was crooning to the tadpoles when this whole business began. It was the same song Mrs. Tuggle sang to Stevie the night Mom and Dad were out of town. I could hardly remember any of it. And Mouse, I was so *glad.* I was thinking that maybe, slowly, all of this would fade away and we'd be normal people living in a normal house in a normal Indiana town. And then, last night, all the words of all three verses came to me as clearly as if someone was playing a record. I don't mean in my head, remembering. I mean in my ears. I *heard* them, Mouse."

"Maybe someone *was* playing a record," Marjorie suggested. "Maybe the song's on tape, and that's where they learned it in the first place. Are you sure Judith wasn't playing it over on her side of the bedroom?"

"Judith was sound asleep, Mouse."

Marjorie thought some more. "Well, maybe it's in her unconscious, and she was singing the words in her sleep."

"Mouse, it all started in the kitchen! Just a whisper, so faint I could hardly hear it. It wasn't Judith's voice, either."

"W-whose was it?"

Lynn couldn't answer. Couldn't bring herself to say the word. "Hers," she said at last.

Mouse stole a sideways glance. "Mrs. T's?"

Lynn nodded.

"Oh, Lordy!" breathed Mouse. They reached the school and went in.

All through English and social studies, Lynn found herself glancing toward the windows of the classroom. All she needed to see now, she thought, were the nine crows gathering, watching her, following her and Mouse wherever they went. All it took was the return of Mrs. Tuggle's demon cat, and she would know that things were beginning all over again. But the branches held nothing but buds and an occasional sparrow. Everything had a green, feathery look. No crows. No cat. Just a cold spring sky.

"Something interesting out there, Lynn?" the teacher asked as Lynn noticed an awkward silence in the room, then a giggle.

"No, ma'am," she said quickly, turning her attention to the blackboard, where the teacher was listing all the presidents and vice presidents.

"Abraham Lincoln," said Mrs. Edmunds, "paid attention." It was exactly the kind of thing Mrs. Edmunds would say.

At recess, Mouse edged Lynn over toward the fence, away from the soccer game someone had started. "I think I know what you should do," she said.

"About the whispers?"

Mouse nodded, her glasses slipping down a little on her nose. "Ignore them. Just ignore them. Don't get involved. That's the way to handle witchcraft. If it's around, if you even *think* it's around, just don't get caught up in it. Don't even think about it. If you don't listen to the whispers, they'll go away."

Lynn could hardly believe that this was Marjorie Beasley talking. She sounded more like Lynn's father.

"Listen." Mouse grabbed her arm. "Do you remember that night at my house, when we were alone? And the cats and crows were outside? And we heard Mrs. Tuggle's voice singing? Remember what we did?"

Lynn thought, then remembered. "We sang the song too. We sang it as loud as we could, *screamed* it, even. And we stopped her singing."

Mouse nodded emphatically. "Beat her at her own game. Sing it right back at her, as loud as you can."

"I thought you wanted me to ignore it."

"Well, ignore it first, but if that doesn't work, then sing it. Two can play her game."

They sat down on a wall at the end of the field. The sun had just poked through the cloud cover, and felt warm and comforting on their thighs.

Lynn felt comfortable outside, but not inside. "Do you know what you just said, Mouse?" she asked finally.

"What?"

"You said *her.* 'Two can play *her* game.' Like she's here. Like she's back."

Mouse hugged herself with her arms.

This time Lynn's voice sounded small and soft and scared. "What are we going to do, Mouse?"

There was no answer. Mouse sat like a statue, staring out over the playground at the soccer game.

"How do you do it?" Mouse asked finally, answering Lynn's question with a question of her own. "How do you get rid of a witch?"

"Maybe it's not her exactly that's left behind, but her evilness. Just like Mother always says about goodness: She says that the good you do lives on after you die. Maybe the same is true for evil."

"So just don't get involved!" Mouse said again, going back to her earlier suggestion. "Ignore it. Pretend it isn't there."

"I'll try," Lynn promised. Then, just as the bell rang, she said, "Mouse, tell me the truth. Do you think I imagined it?"

Mouse didn't even hesitate. "No. I know you that well, Lynn. *I* might imagine something that isn't there, but you wouldn't."

It was good to have Mouse around. *Wonderful* to have her. Lynn felt that if she had to keep all this locked inside herself she would burst. She knew that this news about the whispering was about as welcome as chicken pox, but even then, Mouse would rather be told than have it kept from her.

The Morley house, like all the others on the street, was big and rambling, with gables at the top, a bay window with stained glass inserts, and a porch that ran the width of the house. As Lynn approached it that afternoon, she was enveloped in the wonderful smell of cookies baking, oatmeal with chocolate chunks, her favorite kind. Mother was standing by

the table in her slacks and shirt, sliding each cookie
off with a spatula, and she was smiling. Lynn could
hardly believe it. Pancakes for breakfast and cookies after school. Just like the families on television.
Just like the mothers who had nothing more to do
than listen to every little worry their kids might
have.

"Go ahead," Mother said. "Help yourself."

"Oh, Mom! You know how much I like these."

"I thought you would. It's *time* we had cookies in
this house again. The homemade kind."

Lynn settled happily down at the table with a
glass of milk and a large cookie, still warm, that
curled over in her hand. She wanted to capture this
moment and hold on to it. A moment like this in the
kitchen with Mother could put a sort of protective
fence around her, keep other things out. What
other things? Lynn concentrated hard on the taste
of melting chocolate in her mouth and pushed
thoughts of witchcraft out of her head. *Don't get
involved. Ignore them,* Mouse had said.

"I've been hearing a lot of hammering today,"
Mother said as she dropped spoonfuls of dough on
another pan to go in the oven. "Someone said that
builders are putting up a new house where Mrs.
Tuggle's used to be. I'm glad."

"So am I," said Lynn. A new house was even better than just an empty hill. It would help them get
over the memories more quickly. Should she ask
her mother more? she wondered. About what she
thought of all that had been happening here in the
neighborhood? She stole a look at her mother, at

her freshly shampooed hair. No, Lynn decided, she wouldn't risk it. When Mother was ready to talk about it, she would. Meanwhile, Lynn would wait.

She waited now, helping herself to a second cookie. And finally Mother said, "I think this has all been hard on Stevie. He's certainly been cross and out-of-sorts lately. I thought the smell of cookies baking would bring him down here, but he's been playing up in his room since lunch."

"It'll be better when he's in first grade," Lynn suggested. "Once he gets home from kindergarten at noon, he doesn't have anyone to play with for the rest of the day."

Mother leaned against the counter. "I don't know. I can't help but think he's still angry with me."

"For what?"

Mother hesitated. "For spending so much time in my room lately. Well, I'm getting over it now. Every morning when I get up, I say, 'Sylvia, that's all behind you now. Write a new book, a funny one.' And I've got some ideas."

She didn't, Lynn noticed, say, "I'm *over* it now." Only, "I'm *getting* over it," meaning she was still wrestling with the old feelings; meaning, *Lynn, don't bring it up, please.* She wouldn't, Lynn decided. She'd do everything she could to get her mother and the Morley family back to normal.

"Well, I'll go find Stevie and *take* him a cookie," Lynn offered. She put one on a saucer and headed upstairs.

Stevie was sitting on his toy chest by the window. He looked a little like Mother. Both he and Judith resembled Mrs. Morley—their faces round, their blue eyes wide apart. He had a Tinkertoy stick in one hand, and was poking at a dazed fly—either a leftover from last fall, or one of the first of spring—that lay lifeless-looking on his window sill, making a feeble buzz when it was touched, then rolling over and playing dead once again.

"Look what I've got for you!" Lynn said. "Oatmeal-chocolate."

"I don't like oatmeal," said Stevie, concentrating hard on the fly.

"With chocolate chunks in it? Big pieces of choco- late melting in the middle?"

Frowning, Stevie reached for the cookie, dug out all the chocolate pieces, and left the rest on the sau- cer.

"So, how was kindergarten today?" Lynn asked. And when he made no answer, she said, "Next fall you'll be in first grade, Stevie. You can walk to school with me in the mornings and walk home with me in the afternoons if you want to."

"I don't want to," Stevie said. "You always walk with Mouse."

"Well, you can walk with us tomorrow morning if you want."

"I don't want." Stevie poked at the fly again. The fly climbed halfway up the windowpane, then fell to the sill again.

"Want to go down and help Mom bake the rest of the cookies?"

"Nope."

"Want to play "Chopsticks" with me on the piano?"

"Uh-uh."

"What *do* you want to do, then?"

Stevie just laughed. He picked up one of his blocks, a long brown rectangular block, held it up in the air with his left hand, then brought it down as hard as he could on the fly.

"This!" he said gleefully, and lifted the block. There was only a red and black smudge where the fly had been.

chapter three

Lynn sat down in her favorite place in the old cemetery—on the tombstone of Mrs. Elfreda Lewis, which had fallen in front of the tombstone of Mr. Lewis. Mr. Lewis made a marvelous backrest.

Mouse, however, liked sitting between two angels who were holding a book. Mouse sat on the book. This used to be her *very* favorite sitting place until she discovered it belonged to the grave of Mrs. Tuggle's brother. Was supposed to be the brother's grave, anyway, until the city discovered that Bertha Voight was buried there. Mouse would have chosen another place to sit, but nothing was quite as comfortable as the book and the angels, so she stayed.

The cemetery had been the girls' private talking place long before the scary business with Mrs. Tuggle began. Now the city had started moving coffins and tombstones to the new cemetery on the other side of town, and soon this place would become a park. So on this gorgeous April Saturday, while these tombstones were still here, the girls stretched out their legs and tipped their heads back to enjoy the first warm breezes of the season.

"On a day like this," Lynn said, "I think maybe I imagined the whole thing. The whispers, I mean. On a day like this, I figure there just *can't* be witches." And when Mouse made no reply, Lynn added, "Except that I *did* hear the whispers and I know I'm not nuts. I only heard that song twice, Mouse. The first time was when Judith was crooning to the tadpoles last spring down at Cowden's Creek. And then it was only the first verse. The second time I heard it was the night Mrs. Tuggle took care of us when the folks were gone. She sang it to Stevie. I couldn't possibly have memorized all the words, yet I heard all three verses the other night."

"This wasn't the same song we heard her singing the night we were alone at my house?"

"No, I think that was another song."

"Well, say this one to me. What are the words? Can you remember them now?"

"Something about 'shadows of the pool,' and 'dark as gruel.' Or maybe it was 'thick as gruel.' And something about a tea kettle and a bell. No, I can't remember the rest. I couldn't begin to put things in the right order."

"That proves it, then," Mouse said. "You really did hear someone singing that song."

Lynn squinted up at the sky. "Unless," she said, "after hearing Mrs. Tuggle sing it through to Stevie, the words got imprinted on my brain, and there was something about being alone in the kitchen, with the rest of the house dark, that reminded me of that night and brought the words back to me."

"Do you really think that?" Mouse asked her.

"No."

Mouse wrapped one arm around the neck of one of the angels and the other arm around the second

angel. "Why don't I stay at your house tonight, and we'll go down to the kitchen after everyone else has gone to bed and see if *I* hear anything."

Lynn didn't answer right away. She wanted desperately to say yes. With all her heart, she wanted to know if she was hearing voices or if the whispers were really there. At the same time, she wondered if it was fair to get Mouse involved again. There had been a time when Mrs. Tuggle seemed to be trying to get Mouse into witchcraft, and Mouse had been so weak at the time, so vulnerable, so needing a mother to look after her, that she almost came under the old woman's spell. Lynn had no wish to start all that again.

But now, with Mrs. Tuggle dead, it seemed worth risking. *"Would* you?" she said.

"We'd better tell my dad," Mouse said.

They were in no hurry to get up, however. Lynn felt the breeze blow through her hair—a warm, gentle breeze that spoke of summer and flowers and vacations and fun. When she opened her eyes to the sky above, the clouds were puffy, and new leaves decorated the tree branches. There was a crow in one of the trees, but he was paying her no attention at all, and finally flew off. A sparrow took its place, then a robin. Lynn felt strong inside. Mrs. Tuggle was gone, and whatever evil she might have left behind, Lynn could handle.

They got up at last and rode their bikes into town to Beasley's Book Shop. Inside, the shop had the smell of old paper and glue, of ink and worn leather chairs. Of dust and furniture wax.

Marjorie's father was standing behind his desk, sorting through a box of books that he had bought at an estate sale. There were no new books in the store at all. Most of them stood on dark shelves along the walls or on racks in the center of the floor. But behind the counter was a large glass case containing the books that were very old and very rare. Mr. Beasley kept the case locked, taking a book out only when a customer seriously considered buying one.

"Hello, girls," he said, smiling at them and blowing the dust off a book in his hands. "Why would you want to be inside a musty old bookstore on a gorgeous day like this?"

"We were just riding around," Marjorie told him. "I wondered if I could stay over at Lynn's tonight?"

"Don't see why not, if you've finished your Saturday jobs," her father told her.

"I already scrubbed," Mouse said. "I put the dishes away, made the beds, and vacuumed the rug."

"Good girl," said her father. "Go on, then, and have fun."

As the girls started back outside, Lynn tugged at Marjorie's sleeve. In the far corner of the glass case was another copy of *Spells and Potions,* the same as the one the demon cat had destroyed some weeks back.

"Mouse, *where*—?"

"We just got it in yesterday. It's one of the last remaining copies in the world," Mouse told her. "Dad was so upset when Mrs. Tuggle's cat tore up the other one that he won't let this one out of the case."

"Well, let's hope we never need it," Lynn said, and they went to Marjorie's to collect her things. It was comforting, however, to know that the book was there—that at least one other person, more than a century ago, had believed enough in the existence of witchcraft to have written a book about it—how to recognize witchcraft and protect yourself from it.

"Toothbrush, pajamas, comb, socks—what else?" Mouse asked, throwing stuff into a bag.

"A game or something?" Lynn suggested.

"I won't feel like playing it," Mouse said. "I'll be too nervous."

The girls rode to the Morleys' and parked their bikes behind the house.

"Mom?" Lynn called. "Can Mouse stay over?"

"Sure." Mother answered from the couch, where she sat with a clipboard on her lap and papers on either side of her. "What would you like for dinner, Marjorie? Spaghetti or chicken?"

"Spaghetti," Mouse answered.

"You got it," said Mother. She put her pen to paper again, still smiling, and went on writing.

As the girls went upstairs, Mouse said, "She's certainly different, Lynn. She's so cheerful now."

"And I mean to keep her that way," Lynn said. "I don't even mention Mrs. Tuggle to her, and I won't. If we ever talk about it again, it will have to start with her."

Lynn stuck her head in Stevie's door as they

passed his room to see if he wanted to play Old Maid, but he was out, so the girls went on up to the third floor. Lynn pulled out the trundle bed from beneath her own.

"What's Judith doing these days?" Mouse asked.

"Waiting for summer so she can make strawberry jam. It's so *nice*, Mouse, to have Mom and Judith normal again. You just don't know."

Mouse plopped down on the trundle bed. "I'd give anything just to have my mom back, normal or not."

"Oh, Mouse, I'm sorry." Lynn sat down beside her and slapped herself on the mouth. "I just don't think before I say something."

"Well, at least she's not dead or anything. At least I get to see her for a week this summer."

"It'll be a wonderful week," Lynn assured her. "You'll see!" She waited for what seemed like an appropriate length of time, then tucked her legs up under her. "Now, we've got to plan this," she said. "I doubt we'll hear that singing until everyone else has gone to bed. So we'll have to stay awake for a long time, and if Mom or Dad hears us going up and down the stairs, we'll have to have an excuse."

"That's easy. I'll be hungry," Mouse said. "I'm always hungry."

At the table that night, Mrs. Morley put a big bowl of spaghetti in the center, plus some salad, some applesauce, and some garlic bread. Stevie helped himself to a large portion and enjoyed sucking the long pieces of spaghetti noisily into his mouth.

"Stevie!" said his father gruffly. Then, turning to the others, "Anything interesting happen today?"

"I saw Ken Phillips at the mall and he bought me a Pepsi," Judith said.

"I got a whole chapter done on my new novel," Mother told them. "It's going to be a *funny* book this time. I'm calling it *Grandma and Grasshoppers.* It's based on a story my grandmother told me about a plague of grasshoppers in Kansas when she was a little girl, and how they even got in the clothes the family was wearing."

"Yuk!" said Lynn, and she and Mouse and Judith laughed.

"I don't think that's very funny," said Stevie.

"You don't? What do you think would be funny?" Mother asked.

Stevie slurped another long strand of spaghetti into his mouth despite his father's frown. "If all the grasshoppers got their wings took off and couldn't fly."

Everyone looked down the table toward Stevie.

"Why would that be funny?" Lynn asked him.

Stevie started to grin, and spaghetti sauce oozed out of one corner of his mouth. "Because they'd all try to fly, and they'd just go . . ." He plopped one hand on the table. "Wham!"

Mr. and Mrs. Morley exchanged glances and the meal resumed.

After supper, Mother let Judith use some blueberries from the freezer to make jam, and Lynn and Mouse helped. Lynn noticed the way Mouse enjoyed Judith's praise when she did something well.

Everybody, it seemed, was a mother-substitute for Marjorie: Mrs. Morley, Judith, teachers at school, and even—when she was alive—Mrs. Tuggle.

Mouse and Lynn were practicing headstands later on the rug on Lynn's side of the third-floor bedroom when Stevie came up.

"You want to learn to stand on your head?" Lynn asked.

"Uh-uh." Stevie sat down on a chair by the window.

"Want to learn to stand on your feet?" Mouse joked.

Stevie glared at her.

"What *do* you want to do, Stevie?" Lynn asked. "Play cards? Monopoly? Pick-up Stix?"

"Pick-up Stix," he said.

Lynn got down the box from the game shelf and the three sat down in a circle on the floor. Mouse went first and got four sticks. When it was Stevie's turn, he moved a yellow one on his second try.

"You moved one, Stevie," Lynn said gently.

"I did not."

"Yes, you did," said Mouse. "I saw it too."

"*I* didn't see it!" Stevie yelled.

"Well, okay. One more try," Lynn told him.

Stevie tried again and got a red one. Then a blue one. But when he tried a third time, several sticks moved.

"You moved some," Mouse told him.

"Did not!"

"Don't cheat, Stevie," Lynn chided.

"I didn't move any!" he bellowed.

"Yes, you did. We both saw!" said Mouse.

Suddenly Stevie grabbed all the sticks on the floor and thrust the points into Marjorie's arm. She shrieked.

"Stevie!" Lynn yelled, grabbing his hand and holding it. "What's the *matter* with you? You apologize! That was awful!"

"I won't!" Stevie yelled.

"Well, you can't play up here with us, then. Go downstairs," Lynn ordered.

Stevie flung the sticks all over the bedroom, then bounded out the door and clattered downstairs.

Lynn looked at the pricks on Marjorie's arm. One was so deep it had drawn blood. "Mouse, I'm so sorry! He's been acting terrible lately. I'll get some Bactine."

She swabbed her friend's arm and put a Band-Aid on the place that was bleeding. There were tears in Mouse's eyes.

"That really hurt!" she said.

"I'm going to tell Dad," Lynn promised. "Mom says Stevie's been upset with her because she was moody for so long. But he's not just taking it out on Mom. He's taking it out on everyone. I think Dad ought to talk to him."

"It's okay," said Mouse. "I'll live."

The girls went downstairs to watch TV, but mostly they watched the clock, waiting for everyone else to go to bed.

The problem with Saturday night, however, was that no one went to bed early. Even Stevie stayed up until ten o'clock, Judith watched a rerun of *Sat-*

urday Night Live, and Mr. and Mrs. Morley went to
a movie and got in about eleven-thirty. By the time
everyone was in bed at last, Mouse was so tired she
could scarcely keep her eyes open. The girls went
down to the kitchen for some milk and peanuts
around one, but there were no whispers, no singing, no sound at all. They didn't try again.

It was the dream Lynn had that night that was
upsetting. She had been sitting out in the backyard
when she noticed something flying about, a few feet
above her head. She had looked up to see that it was
Stevie—that he had wings of some sort, and was
circling, laughing, then diving at her. She had swatted him away. He came back, however, and this
time the wings had little points on the ends that
scratched her head as they passed. Angrily she had
reached up with a book and hit him. Stevie had
fallen, the wings had come off, and then he began
to decay in front of her eyes. His face began to
shrivel and rot, and Lynn woke in a cold sweat, her
heart pounding, and slept no more that night.

chapter four

It was the next day, after Marjorie had gone home, that Lynn had a talk with her father. The air was unusually warm, the sun bright, and Mr. Morley decided to read the Sunday paper on the porch.

"Hi, Snicklefritz," he said when Lynn sat down on the glider beside him, handing her the comics section.

Lynn spread the comics across her lap but didn't read them. She was trying to figure out exactly which words, in what order, she should use to ask her question. Everything she thought of, however, seemed wrong, sounded too alarming, and the more she tried to arrange the words in her head, the more tangled they became. Finally she just asked the question outright.

"Dad, I was wondering, is there any history of mental illness in our family—either on your side or Mom's?"

Lynn's father closed his eyes and let out his breath. "For Pete's sake, Lynn, it's a gorgeous spring Sunday, I'm enjoying my newspaper, and you're playing psychiatrist again. Can't you at least wait until you get through medical school?"

Lynn stood up. "Just forget I asked, okay? Come to you anytime, you said. Ask anything I want as long as I stick to facts. I only asked a simple question, requiring a yes or no answer, and if . . ."

Father reached out and gently pulled her back down. "Okay, kitten, okay. I'm sorry, I did say it, and I meant it. As far as I know, there is no mental illness on either my side or your mother's—not in the last couple of generations, anyway."

"Okay. Thanks," Lynn said.

"Now may I ask *you* a simple question?"

"Yes . . ."

"Why did you want to know?"

"Because Stevie has been acting positively weird. *Awful.* He stabbed Mouse with a bunch of Pick-up Stix and wouldn't apologize. He's becoming a brat, Dad, and I don't exactly want to tell Mom about it."

"Why don't you want to tell your mother?"

Lynn pressed her lips together. "I can't tell you."

"*Why* can't you tell me?"

"Because I'd have to talk about you-know-what again."

"So go ahead. As long as you stick to facts."

"Okay." Lynn settled back against the glider and began pushing her feet on the floor. Dad put his newspaper aside this time and gave her his full attention. Maybe, at last, they would have a real conversation—heart to heart.

"What I'm wondering," Lynn continued, "is whether everything that's happened this past year— or *seems* to have happened—or all that I *think* happened—well, I'm wondering if it really did happen or if I'm a little bit nuts. Like maybe it's a sort of contagious disease of the mind that Judith had first, then Mom, then me, maybe, and now Stevie. The only one who isn't a little bit nuts is you, Dad, unless you're a little bit crazy for not believing anything until you can see it happening in front of your very eyes."

"Whoa!" Dad gave a whistle. "You sure dropped a load on me that time, didn't you?"

"You asked."

"Fair enough. What you really want to know, Lynn, is what I think about all that happened with Mrs. Tuggle. Isn't that what you're getting at?"

"Yes." Lynn couldn't believe that they were talking directly about "it"—the subject that had been forbidden, practically, in this house for a year.

"Number one," said Father (being a lawyer, he always numbered things), "I think that Mrs. Tuggle was a very clever and unpleasant woman about whom we will never learn the whole truth. I think she probably lied about the way her brother died. Why, I don't know, unless she murdered him, which, I'll admit, is a possibility. It is a fact that his death certificate was never filed in the courthouse; it's a fact that Bertha Voight's body was buried in his place; and it seems to be a matter of record that Mrs. Tuggle and Bertha Voight were enemies of a sort. I will even go so far as to say that I think Mrs. Tuggle might have been a positively dangerous woman, Lynn. But beyond that, I don't know."

"Meaning what?"

"Meaning that I can't go along with your thinking that the woman was a witch. I'm not even convinced there's such a thing as witchcraft. There are a lot of people in the world who do evil things, but you could hardly call them all witches."

"What about us, our family?" Lynn asked. "If she wasn't a witch, what happened to us, then? How did we get involved in it?"

"She certainly had some influence on your mother and Judith. That much I'll concede. I think that Mrs. Tuggle was a woman who needed to feel powerful, and she felt powerful whenever she was controlling people. Exactly why or how your mother and Judith fell for this, I don't know. But I am *very* glad the woman is gone, to be frank. Judith is certainly back to normal, your mother is much better than she was, and I very much want to keep things this way, Lynn, without stirring up still another batch of trouble."

"You talk as though *I'm* responsible," Lynn told him.

"You're not responsible, but I do think you tend to help things along. You focus on behavior that, if just ignored, probably would work itself out. Listen, sweetie. There are primitive tribes—this is a fact—that actually believe that if someone puts a curse on them, they will die. So when a man is told that so-and-so put a curse on him, he just gives up, doesn't eat, can't sleep, his heart races, and he dies of stark terror. Everyone believes it's the curse. It's not the curse, it's the fear. If you tell yourself long enough that you are under someone's power, you might make it come true, simply because you believe or fear that it will."

Why, Lynn wondered, had her mother married a

lawyer in the first place? Why couldn't she have married an artist or sailor or mountain climber or someone who could see beyond facts, who could sense things that weren't yet there—a picture on canvas, an uncharted sea, the peak of a mountain that always seemed just beyond reach.

"May I ask just one more question, Dad?"

"Shoot."

"Do you believe in love?"

"Well, of course."

"Can you hold it in your hand?"

"Not exactly."

"Can you measure it on a scale?"

"No . . ."

"Can you see it?"

"I see what it can do. I can see the effects around me."

Lynn got up. "Well, so can I. But it's not love I'm talking about." And Lynn left the porch and went upstairs.

Who was right, she or her father? Both of them made sense. You could argue either side. She could well imagine how someone like Mouse, for example, might fall under Mrs. Tuggle's spell merely because she thought she was weak and couldn't resist. Something like that didn't have to be witchcraft at all, just a girl wanting a mother. But if Mr. Morley believed in love because he could see its effects around him, Lynn, by the same token, had to believe that there was something else, something evil in the world, when she saw *those* effects around *her*. If it wasn't witchcraft, it was something close.

She lay on her back on her bed, staring up at the sloping ceiling. She shouldn't have walked out on her dad, she was thinking. He had been talking to her just as she'd always wanted. Maybe she should go back down to the porch this very minute and . . .

"Lynn." Her dad was standing in the doorway. "Let's finish this talk, okay?" His voice was gentle. He came into her bedroom, pulled out her desk chair, and straddled the seat, resting his arms on the back.

"I guess I *do* sometimes believe in things that I can't see or measure," he continued. "But even though things happen sometimes that we can't explain, it's no reason to call it witchcraft. In fact, if we can't explain something, we have to be careful about labeling it at all. Before people understood magnetism, for example, they might have called it witchcraft. And think how silly we'd look if we called it witchcraft now."

Lynn continued to lie on her back, thinking it over. At least he was willing to meet her halfway. At least he was admitting that some things *couldn't* be explained—not in the way people generally explained them.

"Okay, Dad," she said, sitting up. "Then I won't go around calling something witchcraft just because I can't understand it."

"*Good* girl, Lynn! *Now* you are actually talking sense."

Lynn walked over to the chair and put her hands on top of her father's. "But sometimes things happen—*still* happen—that scare me."

"Well, *study* them. Reason them out. Maybe some things can't be explained yet, but most things can, if we think about them long enough."

"And if I study them and still don't have an answer?"

"Then it could be one of the seven wonders of the world or it could be creative imagining. Okay?"

"Okay," Lynn said. She started downstairs and her dad followed.

"Lynn," he said when they reached the bottom and he headed for the porch again. "You're not a little bit nuts, if that's what you're thinking. I think you're a perfectly normal young girl with a curious mind, an observant eye, an ear for the unusual, and an imagination that fills your whole head. And I wouldn't change you for the world."

She smiled at him then, and went off to find Stevie.

He was at the kitchen table finishing his Cocoa Puffs. Lynn sat down directly across from him, looked into his eyes, and said, "If you ever, ever attack Mouse again the way you did with those Pick-up Stix, I'm going to drag you right in to Dad, Stevie, and you'll really get it. You hurt her; her arm was bleeding."

Stevie lifted his bowl to his lips, drank the rest of the milk in it, then wiped his arm across his mouth. "She was mean to me," he said.

"All she did was point out that you had moved

some sticks, Stevie. We both saw, and you know yourself that you did. If you don't want to play fair, you don't have to play at all. But you're not going to get away with hurting people. Understand?"

Stevie made a face in answer, and Lynn left things there and went on up to her room to do her homework.

She'd done just what her dad said: study it, face up to it directly. She'd been able to confront Stevie herself and tell him just what she thought without bringing Mrs. Tuggle's evil into it. If she started looking at Stevie as under an evil spell, chances are he'd start acting that way. Dad was probably right. People generally live up to your expectations. Stevie undoubtedly *had* been upset the past few months with Mother acting so silent and distant. He didn't know whom he could count on, and it would probably take some time to win back his trust.

"Lynn," said Mother on Thursday, "could you look after Stevie this evening? Your dad and I are invited to a banquet tonight, and Judith is working late with a friend on a biology project. We should be home by ten-thirty or so."

"Sure," Lynn said. The day before had been as normal as it ever got in the Morley household. Judith had been drawing diagrams of a frog's digestive system at one end of the dining room table, Mr. Morley had been studying his legal briefs at the other, Mother had sat in her chair in the living room, clipboard on her lap, writing her new book, and Stevie had amused himself quietly in his room.

At last, Lynn thought to herself, *we're a family again.*

"What do you want to do tonight, Stevie?" she asked him after Judith had gulped down supper and left for her friend's house, and Mother and Dad drove away to the banquet. "We could make popcorn if you want. Fudge, even. With peanut butter in it."

"Fudge *and* popcorn," Stevie said, so Lynn got out the hot-air popper. After the fudge was cooked and cooling, Lynn sat beside Stevie on the couch and read him his favorite Frog and Toad books. But he didn't snuggle up to her the way he usually did.

"You know, kid," she said when they finished one book and picked up another, "I think maybe you could use a bath tonight. And aren't those the same clothes you've been wearing for a week?" She poked at him teasingly. "Isn't that a spaghetti sauce smudge on your T-shirt, the same shirt you were wearing last Saturday?"

He pushed her hand away.

"Tell you what, you go take a bath, get your pajamas on, and then we'll have a piece of fudge and I'll read one more book before you go to bed. Okay?"

Stevie went upstairs.

Lynn picked up her homework again—her diagram of all the presidents and vice presidents, how long they were in office, and whether they died in office or served out their terms. When, she wondered, would she ever have to know this stuff? She wondered if Mom and Dad, when they went to parties, ever sat around talking about how long Andrew Jackson was in office or whether President Harding had served out his term.

It was some time before she realized that she had not heard the bath water running upstairs. Had heard scarcely any noise at all, in fact. She looked at the clock on the mantel. Eight-thirty. She was sure she had sent Stevie up there half an hour ago, at least.

"Stevie?" she called. There was no answer. She decided to finish out the term of McKinley before she went upstairs. It was then she heard it:

> "From the shadows of the pool,
> Black as midnight, thick as gruel . . ."

Lynn froze, fingers rigid around her pen.

> ". . . Come, my nymphs, and you shall be,
> Silent images of me."

"Shut up!" Lynn said, loudly, bravely, to the empty room. But the whisper went on:

> "Suck the honey from my lips,
> Dance upon my fingertips . . ."

Lynn put down her pen and stood up.

> ". . . when the darkness tolls the hour,
> I shall have you in my power."

She started across the living room toward the hallway. The whispers grew louder and seemed to come from above. As she climbed the stairs, Lynn could feel the goose bumps rise on her arms the higher she got, and her knees began to shake:

> "Fast upon us, spirits all,
> Listen for our whispered call . . ."

The whisper became a rasp:

> "Whistling kettle, tinkling bell,
> Weave your web and spin your spell."

Lynn put one hand on Stevie's doorknob. "Stevie?" she said, turning the handle. She could hardly get the door open. At first she thought that he had pushed his toy chest against it, but when she put her shoulder to the door and pushed with all her strength, she finally wedged it open to find nothing behind it at all. Her little brother was sitting across the room on his bed, silently watching.

"What's going on, Stevie?" she asked, and was aware of the tremor in her voice. "Why haven't you taken your bath? You've still got your clothes on."

"Get out," Stevie said, but it wasn't Stevie's voice. Lynn stared. Stevie's lips moved, and the sound seemed to come from his throat, but it was the voice of an old woman, not Stevie's at all.

Shaking, Lynn looked around the room. Stevie's stuffed animals lay in disarray about the floor—a panda in one corner, a bear draped over the arm of

his rocking chair. A clown lay on the rug and a raccoon had been stuffed beneath the dresser. Every single one of them had a Pick-up Stix embedded in its back or chest.

Lynn lost control. "Stevie!" she yelled. "What's got into you? What is happening?"

Stevie's lips moved. "Get out," the voice said again.

Lynn started forward. Stevie leaped up on his bed in his stocking feet, arms bent, as though ready to attack her. But Lynn was too fast for him. As he lowered his head to lunge, she grabbed him, one hand holding the tops of his jeans, the other holding his shirt, and shook him as hard as she could.

"What's *wrong* with you?" she screamed again, shaking him even harder as he kicked, knowing she was handling it all wrong but past the point of caring. Fear and anger mixed together to give her a strength she didn't know she had, and she shook him like a dust mop, then tossed him back on the bed again.

Clunk. Something fell out of Stevie's jeans pocket and hit the floor. Lynn heard it drop, heard it roll. She turned to look, following the small round object as it spun across the hardwood floor and came to rest against a leg of Stevie's dresser.

Slowly Lynn walked over to look. Her knees almost buckled as she bent low, one hand to her throat. It was an eye—a green glass eye, and it seemed to wink at her once in the darkness beneath the dresser before it went dull again.

chapter five

For one brief moment Lynn panicked. She felt her heart race, and all she could think of to do was scream or run.

Then she felt Stevie's head against her arm, Stevie small and quiet. And crying.

"Why are you mad at me, Lynn?" he asked. "Why did you shake me?"

Lynn stared down at him, then at the eye. He seemed a completely different Stevie now, the same little brother she'd always known. Without answering, she put one hand on his head, stroked the back of his neck, and waited until she could talk without gasping.

"I thought I told you to take a bath and get your pajamas on," she said finally.

"I will now," he said, and got his pajamas.

"What happened here?" Lynn asked, pointing to all the animals and the stuffed clown, lying about the room with Pick-up Stix in their bodies.

"They're killed!" Stevie said, as if in surprise. He started around the room, taking the sticks out of his animals, running his finger over each wound, then hugging the toy to him.

"Who did this, Stevie?"

"The bad boy," Stevie said.

"*What* bad boy?"

"Me the bad boy. But the good boy's going to take them all out and make them well." Stevie continued his mercy mission until all the toys had been rescued.

So even Stevie sensed the power inside himself for both good and evil, Lynn thought, just as she and Mouse had discovered when trapped in Mrs. Tuggle's basement. When all the toys had been set on top of the toy chest, Lynn took Stevie's hand and led him over to the dresser.

"What's that?" she asked, trying to sound as calm as she could.

"My marble!" Stevie said, bending down to pick it up, but Lynn held him back.

"Where did you get it?"

"It's mine, Lynn! I found it."

"Where?"

"Up at Mrs. Tuggle's house. After it burned down. Before the bulldozers came. It was lying there in the ashes."

"And you put it in your pocket?"

He nodded.

"And it's been there all this time?"

He nodded again.

Lynn stooped down and grabbed Stevie by the shoulders, her face only a few inches from his. "Listen to me, Stevie. You can't have that. It's not good for you. We have to throw that one away, but I'll buy you a whole bag of marbles to make up for it."

"A green one, just like that?"

"A green one even bigger than that one. Any color you want."

"Promise?"

"Promise. Now, go get your bath and we'll have that fudge."

Stevie trotted off to the bathroom. The door opened without any problem.

With her heart still pounding, Lynn sat down on the edge of Stevie's bed, listening to the water running while she studied Mrs. Tuggle's green glass eye. It had never occurred to her that someone would find it and pick it up, least of all Stevie. Never occurred to her to think of what might happen if that eye was in Stevie's pocket. Now she knew. And though her father might consider it all a coincidence that Stevie's strange behavior of the last week had anything to do with his finding the eye, Lynn was taking no chances. She had to do something with it before Stevie finished his bath.

She would not touch it directly, that she knew. In fact, she would thoroughly wash Stevie's hands again after his bath, and throw his jeans in the hamper. She could pick the eye up with a pair of kitchen tongs, but then what? If she buried it, a dog might unearth it. If she threw it in the fire, it might not, once again, burn. If she took Dad's hammer and tried to smash it, there would be a thousand fine pieces of evil to scatter even farther. What she wanted to do was call Mouse, but there wasn't time.

Lynn went to the kitchen and returned with a pair of tongs and an empty metal box that had held only one last tea bag. Gingerly, she tried to pick the eye up with the tongs, but lost her grip on it. The green eye rolled even farther under the dresser.

Lynn got down on her hands and knees and reached under the dresser with the tongs. In the darkness, the eye winked at her again, as though it were teasing. This time her grip held. Slowly she dragged it out, dropped it in the tea box, put the lid on tight. Then she took it to the kitchen, sealed the lid on with tape, took it to the basement, and placed it on a shelf behind a row of Judith's preserves until she could think of what to do next.

When Stevie came down at last, Lynn washed his hands in the sink.

"We've got to be *really* clean before we can eat fudge," she told him.

She cut them each a large square, took their saucers into the living room, and with Stevie beside her, skin still wrinkled from his bath, one pajama leg sticking to one moist knee, she read him *Frog and Toad Are Friends.* Stevie noisily ate his fudge, while smacking his lips and wiggling his toes with pleasure, and gave her a hug when it was over.

Long after he had gone to bed and the house was quiet, Lynn sat on the couch, in the same position, and thought about what had happened. It wasn't exactly a scientific experiment, she knew, but she would see how Stevie behaved now that the eye was out of his pocket. Already there had been a change.

She would not show the eye to her mother or to Judith. Would not even tell them about it. She imagined taking it to her father, telling him about its being in Stevie's pocket, and all that had gone on in his room.

"Lynn," he would say, "you can't come to any conclusions when something happens only once. You can make a hypothesis about what *might* happen, but you would have to put the green glass eye in the pocket of hundreds of little children, without their knowing what it was. You would have to have people studying these children, as well as another group of children who did *not* have the eye in their pockets, and without the scientists knowing which child did and which didn't, before you could correlate your data and see if the results were statistically significant."

Lynn never understood all of what he meant when he talked like that, but she had heard it so many times she could recite those phrases by heart. *Correlate your data. Make a hypothesis.* She did understand that you had to repeat a study many times. She did understand that you had to compare what happened with another group of people, a control group, Dad called them, who did *not* have whatever it was you were studying—a green glass eye. And she knew that the people who were doing the testing could not know which was which, so that they would not imagine behavior that was not there. That much she did understand. But she also understood that she wasn't about to stick that green glass eye in any other unsuspecting little boy's pocket.

If the evil lived on in Mrs. Tuggle's green glass eye, what could she possibly do with it? The only thing she could think of was to look it up in *Spells and Potions,* back in Beasley's Book Shop. And to do that, she would have to tell Mouse what had happened.

Dad and Mom wouldn't be home for another half hour yet. Lynn went to the phone in the hallway and dialed Marjorie's number.

"Just a minute, Lynn. I can't hear you. Dad's playing the piano. I'll take the phone into the closet," Mouse said. And after a series of thunks and clunks, the music died away and then Mouse's voice was back on the line. "What's up? Did you finish the presidents?"

"No," said Lynn. She realized that her voice was shaking again. Realized, in fact, that her whole body was trembling. Strange how you can go through a terrifying experience and not feel the real fear until later, she thought. It was definitely striking now.

"Lynn?" There was a pause. "Lynn, are you okay?"

"No," Lynn said.

"Where are you?"

"Home."

"Alone?"

"Stevie's here. Mom and Dad will be back in a little while."

"What's the matter?"

Lynn scarcely knew how to begin. She had never mentioned the green glass eye to Mouse. Hadn't even wanted to think of it herself. Now she had to tell her everything.

"Mouse, do you remember that day after the fire

at Mrs. Tuggle's, when we rode back up there on our bikes and walked around in the ashes?"

"Yes . . ."

"Mouse, I—I saw something there. And I didn't tell you because . . . well, because I wanted to forget about it. But just before we rode off again, I saw Mrs. Tuggle's eye. Her green glass eye there in the ashes."

She heard Mouse gasp at the other end of the line.

Lynn started to tell her how the eye had winked at her, then decided to leave that part out. Facts. She would stick only to facts. Maybe she only *thought* that the eye had winked. She couldn't prove it. But she could prove that this was Mrs. Tuggle's green glass eye, if necessary. Everyone knew that the old woman had had one gray eye and one green one, and Lynn had discovered why.

"What did you do with it?" Mouse was asking.

"Mouse, are you crazy? I didn't do anything. I just left it alone."

"And so . . . ?"

"What I didn't know was that Stevie's been up there. He found that glass eye just before the bulldozers came, and thought it was a marble. He's been carrying it around in his pocket."

It was Marjorie's voice that was shaking now. "Oh, Lordy, Lynn!"

"Mouse, I *know* this is why he's been acting so awful. Well, I can't know for sure, but I suspect it. I think this is where the singing's been coming from." And then she told her all that had happened that evening.

"W-where is it now? The eye?" Mouse asked.

"I picked it up with a pair of kitchen tongs, put it in a tea can, taped the lid, and hid it behind Judith's preserves in the basement."

"Are you going to leave it there?"

"Of course not. I don't want it in the house. Somehow we've got to get rid of it in a way it can't turn up again. What we need, Mouse, is to look it up in your father's rare book, *Spells and Potions.*"

"It's locked up!" Mouse told her. "He won't let anyone open that case."

"I know," said Lynn.

They were silent while Mouse thought it over. "I can think of only one way," she said at last. "On Saturdays, he likes me to come in and watch the store while he goes to the bank. He's always gone about fifteen minutes. I know where he keeps the key, but that means we'd have to get the book out, read up on witches' eyes, and get it in the case again before he got back."

"We'll have to try, Mouse. What else can we do? Do you want to just tell your dad about the whole thing and let him decide? Maybe he's not so much on facts as my dad is."

"All my dad will think of is what happened to his last copy of this book when he let us use it," Mouse said. "Dad isn't into witchcraft, Lynn. He's interested in old books about naval battles and the Civil War."

"Saturday, then? Can I stay in the store with you while he goes to the bank?" Lynn asked.

"Okay. He wouldn't care," Mouse said. Then, "Lynn, are you scared?"

"Petrified."

"Do you think it's all happening again?"

"Not if we can get rid of that eye. But we've got to do it right this time."

The following day, Stevie came down to breakfast all smiles. He wore a clean pair of jeans and a clean shirt and ate his cereal politely. He told Mother how he and Lynn had made fudge and popcorn, and seemed to have no memory at all of what had gone on in his room. Made no mention of the marble in his jeans or the sticks in his stuffed animals.

"Well, your dad and I had a nice evening too," Mother told him. "It was fun to get out again and go someplace. We've got to do that more often."

That afternoon, Lynn and Mouse stopped at the five and dime after school and bought Stevie a new bag of marbles, including a huge green one with a white center. Stevie was delighted.

"We're going to go about this scientifically, Mouse," Lynn told her as they sat on the cushioned window seat in the music room. "We aren't going to imagine anything. We are simply going to read up on how to get rid of a witch's eye, do it, and that's that. That will be the end of it."

"You hope," said Mouse.

"What else can we do?"

The entire Morley family came to dinner that evening in a good mood. Mr. Morley had won a case in court, Mother had finished another chapter of her book, Judith announced that she and her friend had received a B+ on their biology project of a frog's digestive system. Lynn said that she had made six out of ten baskets in basketball in gym, and Stevie showed off the new marbles Lynn had given him, without mentioning the one she had taken away.

So far, so good, Lynn thought.

It was then it happened. The crash in the basement.

"What was that?" Mother said, scooting back her chair.

"A robber?" Stevie cried.

"That was certainly the sound of breaking glass," said Mr. Morley.

Everyone went to the basement, Judith in the lead. And then Lynn heard her sister scream. When she reached the bottom step, she saw that the shelf holding Judith's preserves had fallen, and there was broken glass and jelly all over the basement floor. In all the confusion, no one noticed the tea can which lay off to one side. No one but Lynn.

Judith was sobbing. "All that *work,* Mother! I've spent hours making jam, and now this!"

"I really can't understand it," said Father, examining the shelf support that had given way, pulling the screw from the wall. "I was sure I had put this up securely."

"What a shame!" Mother was carefully picking

through the mess on the floor to rescue the two or three jars that remained unbroken. "Judith, I think I still have some blueberries left in the freezer. If you want to try again sometime, I'll show you how to make freezer jam. It's a lot easier, and tastes even better than canned preserves."

"A river of jelly!" Stevie pronounced, gingerly stepping back and forth across the stream of preserves on the floor.

Unnoticed by the others, Lynn picked up the tea can with Mrs. Tuggle's eye in it, took it upstairs, and put it beneath her bed.

chapter six

"Mouse," Lynn said on the phone the next morning. "Come over."

"I thought we were going to my dad's bookstore."

"We are. But stop by here first."

In minutes there was the squeak of Marjorie's bike outside, a thud against the side of the house, and then footsteps on the porch. Lynn met her at the door.

"Who died?" Mouse asked. "You look awful!"

"Judith's preserves, that's what. All over the basement floor."

"What happened?"

Lynn grabbed her arm and pulled her upstairs. When they got to Lynn's bedroom, she said, "Listen, Mouse, it's where I hid the eye. Remember?"

Marjorie sank down on the edge of the bed. "The eye got out?"

"No, it's still in the tea can, and the lid's taped shut."

"Then how—?"

Sometimes Mouse was maddening. "What difference does it make *how*? I don't *know* how! It doesn't have to get out to do its damage. It just has to *be*!"

"Where is it now?"

"Under the bed."

Mouse leaped up and flew halfway across the room. When she had finally caught her breath, however, she said, "Let's see it."

Lynn looked at her. "Are you sure?"

"Just a peek."

Lynn crawled under the bed, retrieved the tea can, and the girls sat down on the rug. Carefully Lynn pulled off the tape on either side, lifted the lid, and looked. The green glass eye winked at her from the bottom of the can.

Without a word, she passed the can to Marjorie. Mouse stared into it for a few seconds, then her mouth dropped. "It—it *winked* at me, Lynn."

"I know." Lynn felt enormously relieved. She *wasn't* crazy. She didn't just imagine that the eye had winked or blinked or whatever. It really happened.

She took the can back and taped the lid on once more. "Let's go to the bookstore and see if we can find out what to do with an eye."

"Are you sure it's safe to leave it here while we're gone?"

"I'm not sure of anything, Mouse. What else can I do with it? If it made the shelf collapse, maybe it will make my bed collapse, and if the bed falls down, I hope it smashes the can and the eye to smithereens."

The sky was overcast and chilly, not sunny like the week before, and Lynn was glad when they reached the bookstore, chained their bikes to the bench out front, and went inside.

"Anything I should know before you leave, Dad?"

Marjorie asked her father as he prepared to take his weekly earnings to the bank.

"Just be helpful and answer questions," he told her. "You know how to operate the cash register if you need to. We have a gentleman browsing there at the back, and two women over in the poetry section."

"Okay." Mouse sat down on the stool behind the counter, but Lynn's eyes were on the glass case behind it, with the rare books inside. On the second shelf of the case was one of the world's last remaining copies of *Spells and Potions.*

Lynn watched, curious, while Mr. Beasley took off his suit jacket and put on an old grubby sweater instead. He took off his reading glasses and put on dark sunglasses in their place. Then he took the canvas money bag from beneath the counter, dropped it in a Wonder Bread sack, picked up a Thermos, and walked out the door.

"It's his disguise," Mouse explained.

"But if a robber catches on, he'll simply look for a man in a sweater, holding a Wonder Bread sack," Lynn said.

"He changes every week," Mouse told her. "Sometimes he wears a cowboy hat and carries a briefcase; sometimes he doesn't wear any hat and carries a tool box." She got a key from the back of the cash register and unlocked the glass doors of the rare-book case. "Here," she said, handing Lynn *Spells and Potions.*

Heart thumping, Lynn took the ancient book to a chair in one corner. Where to begin? There was no index. The pages were very old and yellow, crumbling at the edges. The print was small and faint, and at the top of each page was a single word, in flowery scroll, telling what that particular page was about. The words at the top weren't even in alphabetical order—words like ASHES, EVIL, WARLOCKS, and ANIMISM. Carefully turning the pages, Lynn looked for either WITCHES, WITCHCRAFT, or EYE, trying to remember where she and Mouse had found the most help before. Probably the section on PO-TIONS, but where was that?

"About ten more minutes," Mouse whispered, walking by. "I'll keep watch on the door."

Lynn finally found the section on WITCHCRAFT, and tried to skim it, but the writing was difficult, and there was certainly no mention of an eye. No, she was going about this all wrong. How many witches had a glass eye, anyway? And of those that did, if there *were* any, how many died in a burning house, leaving nothing behind but the eye? It wasn't the eye that was the problem. It was the evil.

"Five more minutes, Lynn," Mouse warned as she went over to help the two women in the poetry section.

Lynn tried to find the pages on EVIL again. Was that before or after CHARMS? Before or after WAR-LOCKS? Didn't people know anything about alphabetizing back when this book was written?

"He's coming!" Mouse whispered suddenly. "He's crossing the street at the intersection."

By the time Mr. Beasley came through the door again in his dark glasses and sweater, the book was back in the case, the key was back in the cash register, the two women in poetry had moved on to look at books on Victorian furniture, and Lynn felt like crying. It would be another week before she and Mouse had a chance to look in *Spells and Potions* again, and even when they did, there might not be anything that was helpful. A lot could happen at home in a week.

"Thanks, girls," said Mr. Beasley, putting his suit jacket back on again and reaching into his pocket. "You want to stop at McDonald's for a hamburger? Treat's on me."

"Sure!" Mouse said, even though it was only eleven in the morning. Mouse could eat an entire meal every hour of the day and never gain a pound.

They rode their bikes to McDonald's, ordered hamburgers and Cokes, and sat at a table by a window. Mouse wolfed hers down while Lynn chewed thoughtfully, watching the parade of people going by on their usual Saturday morning errands—normal, happy people without any witchcraft to worry about.

"What are we going to do, Mouse?" she said at last.

Mouse stuck the next-to-the-last bite of hamburger in her mouth. "About the eye, you mean?"

Lynn nodded.

"Flush it down the toilet."

Lynn stopped eating and thought about it. She could not understand how Mouse could go on chewing and swallowing and talking about flushing a witch's eye down the toilet all at once. *Nothing* got in the way of filling Marjorie's stomach.

She also had the habit of talking with her mouth full. "That way," Mouse went on, "you won't feel so responsible. The toilet leads to the sewage treatment plant, and that leads to the Wabash River; the Wabash leads to the Ohio River, the Ohio leads to the Mississippi, the Mississippi leads to the Gulf of Mexico, and that leads to the Atlantic Ocean. If the eye gets pounded to a thousand pieces, at least it will get scattered around and the evil will get diluted."

That certainly seemed reasonable, Lynn thought. One little flush of the toilet, and the eye would be gone.

Or would it?

She thought about the time two years ago when Stevie dropped a paper cup in the toilet. A plumber had to come and take apart a pipe in the basement, and there in the curve of the pipe was the paper cup, an old sock, and a couple of Q-tips. What if the eye got trapped in a pipe where no one could reach it? It might not cause any problem with the plumbing, and Lynn would think the eye was on its way to the ocean, when all the time it was there beneath the house. What if the basement walls started to crumble, the floors to sag, and all kinds of things began happening to the Morley house and the people in it? No, she couldn't risk that.

"I can't, Mouse," she said. "If it gets stuck in a sewer pipe, horrible things could happen."

"Bury it," said Mouse, opening a little packet of

mustard, squeezing it into her hand, and licking her palm.

"I thought of that. What else is there left to do? At least then we'd know where it was, in case—"

"And bury it *deep,*" Mouse added. "You don't want a dog digging it up or anything."

When Lynn got home, Mother and Judith were in the kitchen making preserves again. Father had taken Stevie to town for a haircut, and with the rest of the family occupied, Lynn went back outside. She got a shovel and tried to dig a hole by the side of the house in the bushes.

The ground was still hard, however. It was difficult to get the shovel even halfway in, and then Lynn found that roots and rocks were in the way. She decided at last to bury the eye in a far corner of the garden plot, just out of sight of the kitchen window. There the soil was still soft from the yearly digging and spading.

Lynn worked and worked, sweat forming on her forehead. When the hole was two feet deep, she decided that was deep enough that neither of her parents would find it when they came out to prepare the vegetable garden. She went back upstairs for the tea can, put it down in the hole, filled the hole with dirt, and packed it down with her feet. She covered the top with dried weeds and old leaves, then wiped off the shovel and put it back in the shed. *Done.*

The house smelled of preserves. Judith put some on a piece of buttered bread and handed it to Lynn

as she passed. Lynn took it upstairs and sat on her bed, enjoying the taste of warm blueberries. The bed had not fallen down with Mrs. Tuggle's eye beneath it. The room was not in disarray. She felt no presence about her, no remains of evil, and began to wonder if everything that had happened since the fire at Mrs. Tuggle's *could* be explained some other way.

She licked the butter and jam off her fingers and thought it over. It *was* possible that the shelf Father had put up was faulty somehow—a loose nail, a weak support. It *was* possible that Stevie had been acting bad because he missed Mother's attentions, and maybe the attention Lynn gave him the night the eye fell from his pocket, even though she was scolding and shaking him, was enough to make him snap out of it.

What Lynn could not explain, however, in any logical way, was the singing, the force against Stevie's door when she tried to get in, or the strange sound of Stevie's voice.

It's over, she told herself that afternoon when Mouse came by again and they rode up to the school, stopping awhile to join some other girls on the swings, talking of teachers and school, then rode on again.

It's over, she reminded herself again as they rode to the public library, where they parked their bikes and crawled up on the wall beside the front steps. People milled about on the sidewalk below, and

Lynn wiggled her feet in pleasure as the sun warmed her back.

Mouse pulled a pack of gum from her pocket, unwrapped a piece, then pulled it slowly into her mouth with her tongue. "Where is it?" she said.

Lynn took the pack of gum that Mouse was offering. "In the garden," she answered, knowing exactly what Mouse meant.

"Deep?"

"Two feet, at least."

"Was your room okay?"

"Nothing was changed. Everything is back to normal. Judith made more jam, and I really think we've got it under control."

"Good." Mouse chewed noisily on her stick of Juicy Fruit. "Good!" she said again, even more emphatically. "Then we can talk about something else for a change."

Lynn smiled. "Like what?"

"Like what I should take Mom when I visit her this summer. A present, I mean."

It had never occurred to Lynn that when you went to visit a mother who had left the family in the first place, you had to take her a present. According to Lynn's way of thinking, it should be the mother who was giving presents to Mouse—Mrs. Beasley who should be trying to make it up to Marjorie somehow. It was as though Mouse had to thank her for inviting her to visit—bribe her into coming home again. Mouse had been the last child born into the Beasley family; her two older brothers were already married and living in other states.

Lynn wondered if Mrs. Beasley had been planning to leave her husband all along, and when Mouse was born, decided she had to stick around for a few more years yet. Or did the decision come suddenly and take the whole family by surprise? She didn't know, and there was no way she could really ask Mouse.

"What kind of gift did you have in mind?" she asked instead.

"Well, what I was *really* thinking about was taking her a jar of blueberry preserves, like Judith taught me to make. Just to show Mom how much I've learned."

"That would be really nice, Mouse. She'd like that. Maybe you could even teach *her* to make preserves. Judith could give you the recipe, and you and your mother could go shopping for blueberries together."

Mouse grinned wider and wider.

When Lynn got home later, her father was up on a ladder taking down the storm windows.

"Already?" Lynn asked.

"Supposed to get up into the seventies tomorrow," he called down. "I figure we don't have much cold weather left, even if this is a little early. Meanwhile, we'll at least have some cool air in the bedrooms at night." He climbed halfway down the ladder. "Here," he said, handing a storm window to Lynn. "Set that against the side of the house, will you?"

It was a good day to be alive, Lynn thought. Mother and Judith had finished their preserve-making and had gone for a walk; Father was getting the house ready for summer; and on the way upstairs, Lynn stuck her head into Stevie's room to say hello and found him putting Band-Aids on all his stuffed animals where the Pick-up Stix had punctured them. He was kissing each animal and putting it to bed.

"They're all well now, Lynn," he told her.

"That's wonderful," she said.

It was nice to have the storm windows off that night. Lynn and Judith opened windows at opposite ends of their third-floor bedroom, and a gentle breeze blew through, a warm breeze, preparing them for summer.

Lynn let one foot dangle off the edge of the mattress, two pillows beneath her head, enjoying the smell of damp earth and old leaves and spring in Indiana.

"Judith," she said, after her sister's light went out on the other side of the dividing curtain, "when Mouse goes to visit her mother this summer, she wants to take a jar of preserves—some that she's made herself. Will you give her the recipe?"

"Sure. Wait till the strawberries are out in June. I'll give her the recipe and we can even make a batch before she goes." Judith yawned. "Oh, I'm *so* tired! That walk with Mother did it. I'll be asleep in two minutes."

She was asleep in one. Lynn could hear Judith's rhythmical breathing from behind the curtain. She herself lay quietly, drifting in and out of dreams. At last she pulled her feet up under the covers, rolled over on her side, and settled down. The breeze came again. She could hear the curtains flapping now and then when the breeze blew extra strong. And then she heard something else.

Lynn opened her eyes and listened. It was a swooshing, fluttering sound. She raised her head from the pillow and listened intently. The sound grew louder, then receded; grew louder, then softer. The third time, as it grew louder, the fluttering seemed to be coming right at her, and then something grazed her cheek and swooshed on by.

She gave a small shriek and pulled the covers up over her head. On and on the fluttering went and then it stopped as quickly as it had begun.

Lynn lay waiting for her heart to slow down, the pounding to stop. And then there was another sound in the bedroom. *No,* she told herself.

> "From the shadows of the pool,
>   Black as midnight, thick as gruel . . ."

"No!" Lynn said again, this time aloud.

> "Come, my nymphs, and you shall be
>   Silent images of me."

Lynn rolled over on her stomach and buried her head beneath the pillow.

chapter seven

It was a night of fitful sleep. Sometimes when Lynn woke, she thought she heard the singing, sometimes she didn't. If it hadn't been for Judith on the other side of the bedroom, Lynn would have gone to the window and sung the song herself, just thrown it right back out to the wind. But if Judith didn't hear it, and she seemed not to, Lynn wasn't about to tell her.

She was so tired that she slept through the next morning. Mother and Dad, Judith and Stevie, went on to church without her, and Lynn was just coming downstairs when they got home.

"I tried to wake you, Lynn, but you looked so tired," her mother said.

"I'm all right," Lynn told her, and poured a bowl of Rice Chex.

Her father was helping himself to some leftover coffee. "Thought that cool, fresh air would put you right to sleep," he said. Lynn could feel his eyes on her, so she took a chance.

"Something kept me awake," she said. "I kept hearing this whooshing, fluttering noise, and something touched my cheek."

She saw her parents exchange glances, and then Father started to laugh. "I'll bet a bat came in your window," he said. "I'm sure that's what it was, Lynn. Probably went out the same way it came in."

"Ugh," said Mother. "I can do without bats."

"I figured we still had another month before the bugs were out, so I didn't bother to put the screens on," Father said. "I'll put them on soon. That will solve it."

Judith was nibbling on a piece of coffee cake. "Is it true that if a bat gets in your house, it goes right for your hair and never comes out? I heard that once."

Now Mother was laughing. "If that were true, there would be a lot of people walking around with bats in their hair."

"Bats in the belfry," said Dad. "Now, I've seen a couple of people like *that.*" He grinned.

Lynn smiled, too, as she ate her cereal. *Now, think,* she told herself. *The eye is out there, but I'm in here. If Mrs. Tuggle wants to sing, let her. Why should I care?*

She felt better then, but only a little. If an old woman were sitting out in the garden singing, that was one thing. But when a woman's *eye* is out there singing . . .

Lynn did her homework for Monday, made her bed, went for a walk with Stevie along Cowden's Creek to look for cattails, and when Mouse came over later that afternoon, Lynn sat with her in the kitchen while Judith wrote down the recipe for blueberry preserves to take to her mother when summer came.

After Judith left the kitchen, however, Lynn said, "Mouse, last night I heard singing again."

"The *song*?" Mouse asked fearfully.

Lynn nodded. "Dad took off the storm windows yesterday, and Judith and I had the windows open. It was after Judith fell asleep that I heard it."

"What did you do?"

"Put my head under the pillow."

"How grown-up of you, Lynn," Mouse commented.

"What else *could* I do? I couldn't sing it back, not with Judith in the room."

"No, I guess not."

"Why don't we go out to the garden right now, stand on the very spot where the eye is buried, and sing Mrs. Tuggle's song together. Just toss it right back at her."

"I don't remember the words."

"Then I don't even *want* you to know them, Mouse. I don't want you mixed up in this any more than you have to be. Come on. I'll at least show you where it's buried."

They went out the back door, across the porch, down the steps, and out to the garden next to the meadow that led to Cowden's Creek. Lynn could just make out where she had stomped the ground and sprinkled handfuls of weeds.

"Here," she said. "Close your ears, Mouse. I know the first verse, anyway, and I'm going to sing it right now."

Mouse turned her back and put her fingers in her ears. Lynn sang the first verse of the song:

"From the shadows of the pool,
  Black as midnight, thick as gruel,
  Come, my nymphs, and you shall be
  Silent images of me."

"Okay," she said, "I feel better. Come on down to the creek and I'll show you where Stevie and I found cattails."

They opened the gate at the back of the garden and started along the narrow winding path through the meadow.

"It didn't do any good to close my ears. I heard anyway," Mouse told her. "Who do you suppose her 'nymphs' are, Lynn? Is that us? Is that what she's trying to do—make us into witches like her?"

"I guess so." And as Lynn said it, she suddenly remembered the words to the second verse of the song:

> *Suck the honey from my lips,*
> *Dance upon my fingertips.*
> *When the darkness tolls the hour,*
> *I shall have you in my power.*

"I *know* so," she added. "I wish Mrs. Tuggle had never moved here, Mouse. Why did she have to come all the way over from England to settle here, in *our* town, in the heart of Indiana?"

It was a question they couldn't answer. They had reached Cowden's Creek and walked along the bank for a while, picking more cattails for Marjorie to take home to her father. But finally they sat down on a grassy place, leaned back against the bank of dry weeds, and enjoyed the sun and the breeze and the soft trickle of water in the creek. If only she could put the quiet and warmth of the afternoon in her head, Lynn thought. Inside her head it felt all dark and stormy. It was Mouse who brought the subject up again, however.

"Lynn, do you remember that awful day when we were trapped in Mrs. Tuggle's cellar and she was upstairs looking for us? And we heard her coming closer and closer. She was talking to us as though she knew we were there, even before she found us. Do you remember how we took that chalk of hers and drew a circle around us just as she started downstairs, and how she screamed when she saw it? She couldn't cross over."

Lynn swallowed. She remembered, all right. "I never saw her so angry," she said.

"But the worst was . . ."

Lynn knew exactly what Mouse was going to say, but let her finish.

"The worst was when she realized she couldn't get through the circle and she called us by . . . by our 'other' names. I didn't even know I *had* another name, Lynn."

"The name's not important, Mouse. It could have been any name at all. Everyone can be good or evil, and she was just summoning up the bad part of us, trying to get the evil to propel us across the line."

"I wish there wasn't a 'Sevena' inside me, just the same."

"Listen, Mouse, when you think about it, that's

nothing new. You know that you can do something
hateful one minute and something wonderful the
next."

"But to think there's someone—some*thing*
around here—an eye, just waiting to bring out the
evil in us. That's pretty scary, Lynn."

"That's what she wants us to be. Scared. That's
the only way witchcraft can take hold—when
you're feeling weak about yourself. The other part
of us is stronger, Mouse. You've got to believe that.
Let the eye stay out here, that's the way I feel. As
long as it doesn't upset anyone else in the family, it
can stay in that tea can in the garden forever, for all
I care. I'll go walk over it every day. I'll jump on it.
It can't hurt me."

On Monday, the sky was clear and blue, and the
wind rushed the clouds across the sky, leaving little
white puffy trails in their wake. Lynn got an A in
both math and science, and felt quite proud of herself. In basketball at recess, she and Mouse made
nine baskets between them, and when school was
over and they walked back to the Morleys', they
went around the house to the garden first thing.
Lynn sang as they neared the place where the eye
was buried:

> "From the shadows of the pool,
>   Black as midnight, thick as gruel,
>   Don't you tell us what to do,
>   We don't want to be like you."

Mouse laughed aloud. *"You* tell her, Lynn!"

It was then, however, that Lynn noticed Stevie playing with a bucket and shovel near the fence at the back. He was filling his pail with dirt.

"What are you doing, Stevie?" Lynn called.

"Diggin' worms," he said.

"Worms? What are you going to do with them?"

"Go fishing. Dad's going to take me fishing. He said we'd need worms."

"When is he taking you?"

"Someday. I said can we go fishing and he said someday, so I'm digging worms."

Lynn and Mouse both laughed.

"Stevie, you have to dig them just before you go fishing so they'll still be alive," Lynn told him. "If you dug them up now, they'd all crawl away or die before you went fishing. You wait until Dad says he's ready to go, and then I'll help you dig worms. Okay?"

"Okay," said Stevie. He dumped the dirt out of his pail and turned it into a castle there in the garden, sticking little pieces of weeds on the top as flags.

Lynn and Mouse went over to the other side of the garden where the eye was buried. The handfuls of weeds were still there—even Lynn's footprints on the soil above. But the earth on the spot seemed to have sunk down a little since she saw it last.

The girls stared at it a minute or two.

"It's natural," Mouse said finally. "When they bury someone, they always pile the dirt up because they know it's going to sink a little."

"Maybe so," said Lynn.

What surprised her was how the words of the song kept coming to mind. At odd times, when she didn't even know she was thinking of them. At dinner that evening, for example. Lynn had just started in on her mashed potatoes when the words of the last verse ran through her head:

> *Fast upon us, spirits all,*
> *Listen for our whispered call.*
> *Whistling kettle, tinkling bell,*
> *Weave your web, and spin your spell.*

You can keep your stupid bell, you can't trap me in your spell, Lynn said to herself.

"What?" said her father.

Lynn blinked. "What?"

"Your lips were moving. I thought you were talking to me."

"Uh-uh," said Lynn. "Memorizing the state capitals." She hated it when she had to lie to her father. Did she have to lie? Well, how would he have reacted if she'd told the truth, she wondered, and recited that verse in front of Mother and Judith? She knew he wouldn't have liked it at all.

"I had a teacher once who gave us all kinds of tricks for memorizing state capitals," Mother said, passing the lima beans to Lynn. "She recited them in a singsong way like this:

> *"North* Dakota, *Bis-*marck;
> *South* Dakota, *Pierre;*

Ne-*bras*-ka, *Lin*-coln;
Kan-sas, To-*pe*-ka. . . ."

"I hope I never have to learn all that," said Stevie.
"Not for a long, long time," Mother told him.

As the days went on, Lynn convinced herself that
the eye would not, *could* not, bother her unless she
let it. When she heard the singing at night, she
tuned it out, or sang her own version of the song to
herself:

> "You can't tell us what to do,
> We don't want to be like you."

It seemed to work. Mouse was already involved
with packing for her trip to visit her mother. She
wasn't actually putting any clothes in suitcases yet,
but she was deciding what jeans to take, which
shirts, how many school pictures of herself her
mother might like, a sack of her mother's favorite
candy.

Just when Lynn felt that things were going to be
all right, however, and she and Marjorie were getting on with their lives, she realized that every day
for the past week when she came home from
school, Stevie had been playing out near the garden.

"What are you doing today?" she asked him once
when she found him with a pitcher of water at the
back of the yard.

"Watering," Stevie told her.

"Watering what? We haven't even planted the garden yet," Lynn told him.

"All this stuff," Stevie said, pointing to the weeds growing about.

"Those are *weeds,* Stevie! We don't even want them here. When it's time to plant the garden, they all have to come up."

"Why?"

"Because they'd keep the vegetables from growing well."

"Poor weeds," said Stevie, turning the watering can upside down and sprinkling the last of the water on a thistle plant.

Lynn bent down and hugged him. "Oh, Stevie, you're wonderful! You're the same little boy I always loved."

Stevie grinned and hugged back.

But the day after that he was making mudpies in the garden, and the day after that, roads in among the weeds for his Matchbox cars.

"Stevie is obsessed with that garden," Mother said when Lynn came in and put her schoolbooks on the table. "I don't know what it is, but he's out there every afternoon. Almost as soon as he comes home from school, he has a new idea for something he can play in the garden. It's wonderful, because I can keep an eye on him from the window. I almost hate to plant vegetables this spring, he's having so much fun in the dirt."

"He'll find other places to play," Lynn told her, and thoughtfully munched a carrot.

"I wonder if I should move it," Lynn murmured as she and Mouse walked to the Beasleys' house after school on Friday. Mouse wanted to show Lynn the clothes she planned to take along on her trip, to see if she had selected the right colors, the right socks.

"Move what? The eye?" Mouse asked as they went up the steps. "If you moved it out of your yard, Stevie still might be drawn to it. Then he'd be out of sight and you'd really worry. As long as he's only making mudpies or watering weeds, who cares? He's happy."

Lynn looked over the clothes Marjorie had spread out on her bed. "Mouse, your mother would love you no matter how you looked," she said. "What are you going to do? Not wear any of these until summer?"

"I just want to have things ready," Mouse said.

They took a sack of pretzels into the living room and watched a little television, but Lynn's eyes kept returning to the fireplace. She could not enter the Beasleys' living room without remembering the night the girls had been in the house alone, with demon cats and crows trying to scratch and claw their way in.

"Did . . . did your father ever get rid of the dead crow in your fireplace?" she asked finally.

"Of *course*!" said Mouse. "You think we'd want to smell dead bird every time we had a fire?"

"So it's gone, then?"

"Well, sometimes when we open the flue a feather

falls out. There may still be a few feathers caught up there, but the crow's gone."

"Good," said Lynn.

When she got home from Marjorie's, Stevie was out in the garden again, playing with Dad's clippers and cutting some weeds along the fence. What surprised Lynn, though, was that Judith was lying on a blanket on the grass, very near the hole in the garden where the tea can was buried.

"Sort of cold to be sun-bathing, isn't it?" Lynn asked, noticing how Judith had rolled up the sleeves of her shirt, letting the sun tan her arms and face.

"Sun's warm," Judith said lazily. "Might as well get a head start on summer."

Lynn walked on by and glared at the place where the eye was buried. The weeds on top were still undisturbed, but the soil had sunk down deeper yet.

chapter eight

The girls were at Beasley's Book Shop early on Saturday morning so that the moment Marjorie's father left for the bank, they'd be ready to look at *Spells and Potions*.

Mr. Beasley went disguised as a priest this time, with a white clerical collar beneath his suit jacket. As soon as he was out the door, Mouse opened the case behind the counter and handed the book to Lynn.

Lynn had already decided that she would concentrate on the section called EVIL, hoping to find some spell or potion they could use to keep it away. ANIMA, the sections read, FAMILIAS, POTIONS, WITCHES, EVIL.

Again Lynn felt helpless as she saw how many pages were devoted to EVIL alone. How could she possibly read them all in fifteen minutes? Nevertheless, she began:

> *Within each man's heart lies both a basic goodness and an inclination to do evil. In those for whom goodness is foremost, the evidence is a gentle nature, motivated by kindness and generosity toward one's fellow man. But in those for whom evil is dominant, a sinister force seems most apparent, and such creatures tend*

to be quarrelsome, easily provoked, and seeking mischief.

Was any of this even true, Lynn wondered, or was it all superstition? What about a person who had an illness, perhaps, and was always in pain? Meeting him for the first time, people might think that he looked quarrelsome, and he certainly might be easily provoked. But it wasn't evil doing it, it was pain. Did any of this mean any more than what you might find in a fortune cookie?

The book seemed prepared for Lynn's question, because the next paragraph said:

> *In some, however, evil is not readily discernible, and those who at first acquaintance seem passive creatures are, instead, studying the ways of harm. It is equally true that those gentle folk provoked by the vicissitudes of life may also, at times, seem quarrelsome. Thus the usefulness of this book, for herein lie spells and potions that not only protect from evil but will help the bewildered reader to distinguish evil from good.*

She had read only three pages more when Mouse whispered, "He's coming back early!" Once again *Spells and Potions* was put back in the case, the case locked, and the key put back in the cash register.

"What did you find out?" Mouse asked when the girls were outside again.

"That it's hard to tell whether someone is out to do you good or do you in," Lynn said disgustedly.

"What else is new?" They got on their bikes and rode home.

As the days passed, what worried Lynn was that not only Stevie, but now Judith as well, seemed drawn to the garden. If she wasn't exactly *in* it, she was near it. And as the weather grew milder still, Mother was often in the garden too. On weekends, Father got into the act.

This wasn't so unusual, was it? Lynn told herself. Doesn't this happen every year? But she wasn't sure. Mother had even served dinner on the back porch sometimes, just to enjoy the air, she said, and Father got the lawn chairs out and put them under the beech tree so that they could sit outside on Sundays and read the paper.

But it wasn't just the backyard that lured them, it was the garden. Every time Stevie played in the dirt, he got a little closer to the place the tea can was buried. Every time Judith lay out in the sun, her blanket seemed to be placed a little nearer to the eye. Lynn would come home to find Mother wandering aimlessly about the vegetable patch.

"It's still a bit early to plant," she said once to Lynn. "I don't know what it is, but I just seem to want to *be* here. Maybe farming is in my blood."

Father spread lime and fertilizer on the ground, chopping the weeds up with a hoe, then turning the soil over with a shovel. He did not dig deep enough to unearth the tea can, but strangely, when he was through, Lynn still knew exactly where the can was buried. Again the soil seemed to sink a little over the place.

If things had stayed there, perhaps Lynn wouldn't have worried. If the family had simply wanted to be out in the sunshine, getting ready for summer, that wouldn't have bothered her. What was upsetting was that the closer they came to the place the eye was buried, the more irritable they became.

Judith, lying out on the grass in her bathing suit late one afternoon, shrieked angrily when Stevie walked by with his watering can and sprinkled water on her feet. And Stevie, in turn, instead of apologizing, threw the rest of the water on her legs, then yelped as she chased him furiously about the yard.

"*Stop* it!" Mother yelled from her chair on the porch. "I'm trying to finish a chapter, and I certainly don't need any uproar."

Was that the same kind of voice Mother had had before, Lynn wondered, when she was using a room at Mrs. Tuggle's as a studio? When she seemed to snap and snarl at everyone? Or was this a common, ordinary day, in which people naturally didn't get along with each other one hundred percent of the time, and Lynn was attributing perfectly normal behavior to witchcraft? How could she ever hope to be a psychiatrist if she couldn't tell normal behavior from anything else?

The following Saturday, when Lynn once again had *Spells and Potions* in her hands, she came across a short paragraph at the bottom of a page that might, she hoped, prove helpful:

> *There do grow, in sundry places, plants and substances that some claim ward off the evil of*

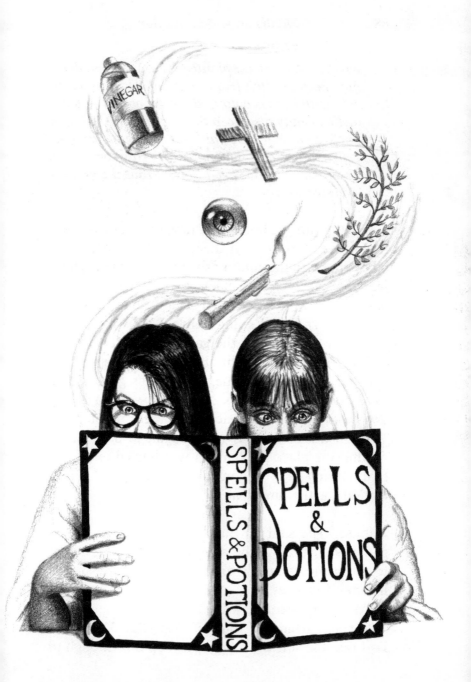

witches. A bay tree, planted near a cottage door, may keep a witch from entering. The mountain ash, with berries coloured red—a colour witches dislike—may also keep the hags from coming in one's door. Similarly dill weed may be used, as well as moss and lichen, which grow sometimes on crosses, for it is well known that the cross is aversive to witches.

When Lynn got home that day, she studied every tree in the yard to see if there might, by chance, be a bay tree or a mountain ash. There was not. There was the beech tree in back, two maples in front, and an elm in the side yard. That was all.

"Mom," she said, going inside. "Are we going to plant any dill weed in the garden this year?"

"Well, I hadn't thought about it," Mother said. "I suppose I could use some, though. It's good in egg salad, delicious in soup. Next time you go to the dollar store, pick up a package of seeds if you like."

There wasn't time, Lynn thought, to plant seeds around the place the tea can was buried and hope that nothing happened meanwhile. She needed protection for the family *now*.

"Mouse," she said on Sunday afternoon as clouds gathered again and the air grew cooler. "We've got to go to the cemetery and scrape some moss and lichen off crosses."

"Moss and *what*?"

"Lichen, whatever that is. Yesterday Mom told Dad that the soil wasn't chopped up fine enough to plant a garden, and Dad snapped at her, said he wasn't the only one with arms and legs, that somebody else could jolly well help."

"So?" said Mouse. "Doesn't anybody in your family have the right to be grumpy? You should have heard my mom and dad argue when she was still living with us."

"But they're not grumpy *inside* the house, Marjorie. It's only when they're near the garden. I'd just feel better if we sprinkled some moss and lichen where the tea can is buried, that's all."

"Okay, let's go," Mouse agreed, and they rode off with a sack and a table knife.

There were five or six crosses in the cemetery, but only two that had anything growing on them resembling moss.

"Excuse me," Mouse said to one of the gravestones, "but could we take some of your lichen?" She looked over at Lynn. "I figure the least I can do is ask."

The formalities out of the way, the girls knelt down by the gravestone and carefully scraped the moss from the cross with the knife blade. They did the same with the second one.

The wind seemed to pick up as the girls got closer to home. The sky was dark, the clouds churning, as though a downpour was due any moment. What surprised Lynn, however, was that after they had parked their bikes by the steps, the wind became fierce, as though they were walking in a wind tunnel. By the time they reached the garden, they had to lean forward to keep going, and when they got to the place where the tea can was buried, Lynn had to stand with her legs apart to keep her balance. Carefully, while Mouse held the sack, Lynn put her hands inside it, carefully lifted the moss, and holding it in her palms, patted it down on top of the soil.

As she did so, she happened to look toward the back porch, and noticed that the bright red pennant Judith had stuck on a post was scarcely fluttering at all, as though this was a demon wind, stirred up by evil, just to keep the girls away.

"Dad," she said that evening, "can there be a lot of wind in one little place and no wind right next to it?"

"Sure." Mr. Morley put his feet on the coffee table and turned a page of his magazine. "Windspouts. You see them all the time in the desert. On the water too. Sort of a miniature tornado."

Coincidence, Lynn told herself.

But it did seem to her that things went more smoothly that week, with the moss from the crosses on top of the tea can. At the same time it seemed terribly superstitious. Lynn had never thought of herself as a superstitious person, and would walk under a ladder just to prove that nothing bad would happen. This, somehow, seemed different.

What if it's all a bunch of mumbo jumbo? she asked herself more than once. If anybody had asked her, before Judith got involved with Mrs. Tuggle, if she—Lynn Morley—would be thumbing through a book on spells and potions, scraping moss from crosses, and burying a glass eye in a tea can, she would have laughed. Was *she* changing?

she wondered. Was the eye beginning to affect her too? And if it was, would she even know it? Maybe. Maybe not.

She didn't go with Mouse to the bookstore the following Saturday because things seemed to be working so well at home. By the time the day was over, though, she wished that she had. Because Mr. Morley went outside to respade the whole garden, just to please Mother. And in chopping the soil up fine, he chopped the moss up, too, and scattered it about—spread it far beyond the spot where the tea can was buried. And coincidence or not, everything seemed to go wrong in the Morley house that night —even *inside* the house.

"Sylvia, I've been working in the garden all afternoon. I'm hungry as a bear, and you give me soup!" Father said.

"It's *potato* soup," Mother snapped. "Potato soup is filling! Eat two bowls of it, if one isn't enough."

"I'd rather have meat, thank you."

"Well, I don't have any prepared, but I *did* spend an hour on that soup, if you'd like to know," Mother answered.

On days when their parents quarreled, which wasn't often, the Morley children sat silently about the table, and their silence always seemed to make things worse.

"If nobody's going to say anything pleasant at this meal, I don't see why we can't take our plates into the other room and watch TV," said Judith.

"So *talk*, if you want to," said Mother.

"There's no point in talking if nobody's going to answer," Judith continued.

"How do you know nobody will answer if you don't *say* anything," Father barked. He took a long, noisy, disgusted slurp of his soup.

"Richard, for heaven's sake! Do you have to eat like that?" said Mother.

"I'll eat my soup any way I please," said Mr. Morley. "You give me soup, I'll eat your soup, but don't tell me how to eat it."

Stevie got up from the table.

"Stevie, you sit right back down here and finish your dinner," said Mother.

"No!" Stevie said, and Lynn wondered if she was the only one who saw his lip tremble.

"Well, if you don't, you're not having anything else before you go to bed."

"I don't *care*!" Stevie said, and ran upstairs.

Spoons scraped, knives clunked.

"Can't you see what's happening to us?" Lynn said finally.

Both her parents jerked their heads up at once.

"What do you mean?" asked Mother.

"Something is making us act this way. The whole family is on edge."

"Lynn, don't *start*!" ordered her father.

"All I'm saying is maybe there's a reason."

"Well, all *I'm* saying is that I'm not going to sit here and listen to any more of this," Judith announced, and took her plate into the other room.

It was awkward, being at the table with Mom and

Dad, neither of whom was speaking to the other. Lynn bit into a cracker, hardly tasting it.

"Oh, to heck with it!" Father said finally, putting down his spoon, and went outside.

Lynn couldn't stand it any longer. She put down her spoon also and ran upstairs. She didn't even bother to turn on the light, just sat by her window and stared out over the backyard, over the garden where the eye was buried.

She saw her father standing on the grass. Saw him thrust his hands into his pockets and pace up and down. And suddenly, he bent over, picked up the shovel he had been digging with that afternoon, and threw it as hard as he could against the back fence.

The next morning everyone slept in. When Lynn got up at last, pulled on her clothes, and went out in the backyard with her grapefruit, she saw that the place where the tea can was buried had sunk lower still, leaving a hole with swirls on the sides. Like a whirlpool, it was sucking her family down into it without their even knowing.

chapter nine

A few days later, everyone in the Morley household was speaking to one another again, and Judith and Stevie, at least, acted as though everything was back to normal. Lynn wasn't sure about her parents. There were times Lynn caught her father looking at her, as though trying to puzzle her out. As though afraid she was thinking about witchcraft again—how to escape it—which of course she was.

"You know what's wrong?" she said to Mouse on their way to school.

"Everything?" Mouse guessed.

"No, not everything. But I just figured it out. The reason Mrs. Tuggle's eye still gets to us is because we're acting as though we're afraid of it."

"Get real, Lynn. We are!"

"But as long as we act as though we're afraid, this will go on and on," Lynn said. "I took it away from Stevie, put it in a tea can, sealed the can with tape, hid it in the basement, then hid it in my room, then dug a deep hole in the garden and buried it. That's acting *crazy*, Mouse. It's just a piece of glass. A simple glass eye. And as long as I act like it's going to scare me to death, it probably will."

"So let's just toss it out and forget about it," Mouse said.

"We can't. We don't have to be afraid of it, but we've *got* to know where it is every minute."

"So why don't you just wear it on a chain around your neck?"

"I won't go *that* far, but I'm going to dig it up, take it out of the tea can, and carry it in my hand to my room."

Mouse stopped walking and stared at her. "Lynn!"

"What's the worst thing that can happen?"

"A wind will blow up and carry you off to Kansas."

"Come off it, Mouse."

"I don't know, but I think you're just asking for trouble."

"All I've had lately is trouble!" Lynn reminded her. "What can be worse than having your parents quarreling?"

"Having your mom move away," Mouse said simply, and once again Lynn felt awful.

"Listen, Mouse, you don't have to touch it, but I just want you along when I dig it up."

"Why? It's only a piece of glass. You said so yourself."

"Mouse . . ."

"Oh, all right, Lynn. I'll go with you. When?"

"After school. When no one else is around."

Sometimes the day seemed to go fast, sometimes slow. There were times Lynn wanted to hurry and get it over with, others when she was terrified of what she was about to do.

The problem was that there *were* people around

just when Lynn finally had a chance to go to the garden. Mother was hanging a bedspread on the line to dry, and Stevie was playing with his Matchbox cars on the back steps. Lynn was all ready to give up when Mother called,

"Lynn, I've got to run Stevie to the doctor for his booster shots. If anyone calls, I'll be back in an hour. Okay?"

Lynn flopped down on the glider and nudged Mouse. "Okay," she said.

Ten minutes later, her mother backed the car out of the driveway.

"Ready?" Lynn asked.

"Can't we eat first?" Mouse pleaded. "One last meal or something?"

"Honestly, Mouse! What do you want? Peanut butter on crackers or Cheetos?"

"Whatever takes longest."

They went inside, and Lynn got out the peanut butter.

It was when Mouse had her mouth full of cracker that they heard the singing. It didn't seem to register on her at first, as though someone were playing a record somewhere. She had finished her last cracker and was picking up crumbs with one finger when suddenly she paused and looked around.

"Where's the music . . . ?"

"It's the singing, Mouse. It's exactly what I heard in the kitchen the night it first began." Lynn stood up and walked slowly around the kitchen. The music was not coming from the stairs this time, it was coming from the kitchen window, which was half open above the sink. Beyond the window, of course, was the garden.

"If you're done, let's go," she said bravely.

"We're going to go out there while she's singing?"

"There isn't any *her*, Mouse. She's gone! She's dead. Whatever's left of her, it's not Mrs. Tuggle."

Mouse swallowed. "Okay. I'm ready."

As they opened the back door and stepped out onto the porch, the singing grew louder.

> "Suck the honey from my lips,
> Dance upon my fingertips.
> When the darkness tolls the hour,
> I shall have you in my power."

"Sing it, too, Mouse! Sing it as loud as you can!" Lynn insisted.

> "Fast upon us, spirits all,
> Listen for our whispered call."

"I—I don't know the words!" Mouse stammered, so Lynn sang for her.

> "We don't want your tinkling bell,
> You can't trap us in your spell."

Lynn finished at the top of her lungs.

She got her father's shovel from the shed, Mouse following behind, and they went into the garden. The place where the tea can was buried had sunk in farther yet.

Mouse stood back while Lynn put her foot onto the shovel and pushed. Strangely, the shovel hardly moved at all. She tried again. It was as though a rock were in the way. It was the same kind of force that had held Stevie's door closed against her pushing. Lynn thrust the shovel as deep as she could, then stood on it with both feet, clutching the handle, and managed to get it down a couple of inches.

Again and again she stood on the shovel, her whole weight pressing down, and little by little the shovel went deeper. Lynn piled the dirt to one side. The singing had stopped, but the wind came again. Mouse's jacket flapped in the breeze as she stood off to one side, hugging herself with her arms.

The wind blew stronger and stronger until it seemed as though Lynn would be blown over backward. Then the shovel struck the tea can, the wind stopped, and Lynn reached down and pulled it out.

"You can't hurt us!" she said, shaking the box determinedly. "We're strong! Mouse and I are strong!"

Squatting down on the grass, Lynn pulled off the tape, opened the lid, and peered down into the can. Mouse was kneeling across from her, hands over her face.

The inside of the can was dark. If Lynn had not heard the eye rattle when she shook the can, she would have been sure it was gone. Then something began to gleam, and before she could change her mind, Lynn thrust her hand inside, grabbed the eye, and pulled it out.

It was icy cold in the palm of her hand, cold and

dead-feeling, yet it seemed to move, to roll, without any motion of Lynn's hand.

> "From the shadows of the pool,
>   Black as midnight, thick as gruel . . ."

Lynn began. Mouse peeped through her fingers.

> "You can't tell me what to do.
> "I am not afraid of you."

The eye winked at her. Lynn put both hands around it and squeezed as hard as she could.

> "You can keep your tinkling bell,
>   You can't trap me in your spell."

She sang out loud and clear. Mouse slowly leaned over to look.

"Do you think she took it out at night?" Mouse said.

"I don't know. Maybe she kept it in and slept with one eye open. Mrs. Tuggle is *gone,* Mouse. This is only her eye—a green glass eye—and if we're not afraid of it, it can't hurt us."

"Well, I'm just glad it's going in *your* bedroom, not mine," said Marjorie. "Where are you going to keep it?"

"I'm going to carry it around with me, that's what. I'm going to know where it is all the time. Then, when I'm out of the house, I won't have to worry whether Stevie will find it. I have a hunch,

Mouse, that if I'm not afraid to carry it, it will slowly lose its power. Whatever evil's left in it will just sort of leak out. But I want you to promise me something."

"W-what?"

"That if I start acting weird, and I don't *know* that I am, you've got to tell me. To stop me."

"If you're acting weird and I tell you but you don't know that you are, you'll never believe me."

"If I don't believe you, take the eye away from me and throw it as far as you can."

"You'd kill me."

"You might save my life."

"You certainly don't *talk* as though you're not afraid of it," Mouse told her.

"Okay, I'm not. As of this day, May fourteenth, at three-fifty-seven in the afternoon, I, Lynn Morley, do hereby declare that witchcraft has no power over me."

Lynn put the eye in the pocket of her shirt, stuffed a Kleenex in on top of it, and Mouse went home to have a snack all over again.

The only thing Lynn noticed was a sensation of cold in the pocket where the glass eye lay. There were times she thought she felt it move against her, but she couldn't be sure. Wearing it next to her clothes as she did, it was easy to imagine things that weren't true. She even put it in the pocket of her pajamas that night when she went to bed, and began writing down in her tablet everything she experienced so as not to miss a thing, so that someday, perhaps, a scientist could take her notes, read them, and say, "This is the first objective account of witch-craft I have ever read."

Sitting in one corner of her bed, Lynn wrote: *I am keeping the eye with me all the time. When I took it out of the can, it felt cold. I don't know if it's unusually cold, or if this is just the way glass is sup-posed to feel. Sometimes, when I know it's in my hand, it seems to move, but it's possible I'm moving my hand and don't realize it.*

There were footsteps on the stairs and Judith came in.

"What'cha doing, Lynn?" she asked, plopping down on her sister's bed.

"I'm just writing things. Sort of a journal."

Judith lay back on the bed, arms up over her head, a contented smile on her face. "Well, if *I* was writing a journal, I would have something wonder-ful to put in it tonight."

"What?"

"Are you ready for this?"

"Ready for what?"

"What I'm going to tell you."

"So *tell* me!"

"Ken . . . Phillips . . . kissed me."

Lynn tried very, very hard to imagine what it was that her sister was feeling. If Judith had said, "I just finished a ten-page report," or "I have just won a hundred dollars," or "I'll never have to wear braces," Lynn might have understood. But the fact that a boy had put his spitty lips against Judith's and held them there did not seem like the kind of thing you could think of for very long without getting a little bit sick.

"He did?" she asked, not knowing what else to say.

"He *kissed* me, Lynn! And I am never going to wipe the place where he touched me."

Now Lynn truly *did* feel sick. "That's sick, Judith," she said.

Judith gave a little laugh. "No, it's not; it's love."

"Oh," said Lynn. "Well, if it will make you feel better, I'll put it in my journal just for you."

Judith closed her eyes. "Write, 'My sister Judith just came into the room with stars dancing in her eyes and announced that she is in love. She was kissed—deliriously kissed—by Ken Phillips, who had both hands on her waist while he did it. "See you around," he said, and squeezed her shoulder.'"

Eyuuuuk! Lynn thought, but she wrote it anyway.

Judith sat up. "I'm going to bed," she said. "If I go right this minute, maybe I'll dream about him, and he'll kiss me all night long, again and again."

"Lucky you," said Lynn.

She could see Judith's silhouette moving behind the curtain. Hear the thunk of her shoes on the floor, the rattle of hangers in her closet, the squeak of the springs as she got into bed.

"Lynn," she said after a moment. "Do you hear voices?"

"No."

"It seems to be coming from your side of the room. I thought maybe you had your radio on."

"No. I don't hear anything."

"It's love, I tell you. I hear music, I see stars, I feel Ken's arms around me. . . ."

"Good night, Judith," Lynn said, shutting her tablet and turning out the light. After a few minutes, however, she asked, "What does the music sound like?"

"Oh, I don't know," Judith answered sleepily. "It's hard to say. Sort of a haunting melody, like an old lullaby or something. I know it's a song I've heard before. Are you *sure* you don't hear it?"

"Positive," said Lynn. "What are the words? Can you make them out?"

"I think it's, 'Sing of morning, sing of noon, Sing of evening's silver moon. Feel the darkness . . . uh . . . touch the black, Hear the shadows whisper back.' What *is* that song, Lynn? It's so familiar. . . ."

"I'm not sure," Lynn told her, but she knew very well. Lynn lay without moving. That was the song Mrs. Tuggle's music box played; she remembered it from the day Mrs. Tuggle invited her and Mouse in for tea, before they knew for sure she was a witch. How could it be that Judith could hear it and Lynn couldn't? That she could be carrying the green glass eye in the pocket of her nightshirt, and still couldn't hear the song?

The eye felt even colder. Lynn shivered and pulled the light blanket up under her chin.

chapter ten

Like something precious she had to protect, Lynn carried the eye with her wherever she went. Except that she was not protecting the eye—she was protecting her family from it.

She had thought that, after a few days of carrying it around, she would forget about it—that it would be like the extra dollar she kept in her shoe for emergencies. But carrying a dead woman's eye—a witch's green glass eye—was something else.

There were times when Lynn was sitting in class that she was sure she felt the eye jiggle. Sometimes it seemed to be growing warmer in the pocket of her jeans—warmer and warmer still—until she felt she had to take it out before it burned her.

Other times it grew colder and colder until her whole body was covered with goose bumps and her teeth began to chatter.

She talked to it. If, when Lynn got home from school, Judith was still out, or was sitting on the porch with Ken Phillips, Lynn would set the eye on the dresser while she took off her jacket and give it a piece of her mind.

"Think you're pretty smart, don't you?" she told the eye once when it almost burned her during a science test. "I'm a living, breathing, human being, and you're just a hunk of glass."

The eye only winked at her.

"I think we've got it licked, Mouse," Lynn said after a couple of days. "I'm sleeping better at night, and I don't worry so much."

"What about the singing?"

"Judith heard some singing one night; it was the tune Mrs. Tuggle's music box used to play, and the words Mrs. Tuggle put to it when she sang the song to us." It was then that a chill raced down Lynn's back. "That's the only worrisome part, Mouse—that Judith heard it and I didn't. Like I'm so used to it that . . . well, that I've become a part of the eye, or the eye a part of me or something. But I don't think so. If this is what it takes to keep my family safe, then I'll carry the eye with me the rest of my life."

"I don't know," Mouse said doubtfully.

But Lynn wasn't afraid. She was beginning to get clever now at thinking up new ways to carry the eye. Sometimes she wore a T-shirt over her jeans and tied a scarf around her waist, the eye secure in a knot at one end of it.

Stevie was his little sweet self again, Judith was wrapped up in daily love notes to Ken Phillips, Mother was hard at work on a new novel, and as long as Lynn kept her worries to herself and didn't bring up the subject of witchcraft, Father seemed relieved that his family was, to all appearances, normal once again.

It pleased Lynn, in fact, that she had the upper hand here, that she could control the eye. She began to feel braver than usual, a bit on the reckless side. Once when Mouse leaned over during math and asked to borrow Lynn's eraser, Lynn slipped her the eye instead, and almost burst out laughing when Mouse gasped and dropped it in her lap.

Another time, she put the eye on Marjorie's tray in the cafeteria, between two butter cookies, and when Mouse, talking to the girl beside her, absently reached down for a cookie and touched the eye instead, she shot Lynn an angry look.

What upset Mouse the most, however, was that the same afternoon in the library, just before the period was over and the librarian was talking about biographies and where to find them on the shelves, Lynn did something really reckless. She and Mouse and a boy were sitting at one of the library tables together near the back of the room. While the librarian talked, the boy left their table and went to sit with friends near the door, leaving Mouse at one end of the long table, Lynn at the other end. And suddenly, Lynn's face broke into a strange smile. She reached in her pocket, took out Mrs. Tuggle's eye, and rolled it slowly down the center of the table toward Marjorie. She smiled even wider when she saw the look of horror on Mouse's face.

"Lynn and Marjorie?" the librarian said, looking right at them. "Are you listening or are you playing?"

"Playing . . . I mean *listening*!" Mouse croaked, her face red with embarrassment as she clamped one hand down over the eye.

"Then would you mind repeating what I just said?"

Mouse sat with her eyes on her hands where the green glass eye was hidden, her face flushed.

"You said that our teachers want a five-page biographical report a week from Monday about somebody other than a president," Lynn responded for her.

"Well, I'm glad that *one* of you girls was paying attention," the librarian said. "There are many interesting people besides presidents to write about, class. Inventors, performers, scientists. Everyone knows who George Washington and Abraham Lincoln were. Be creative. Write about someone else."

Outside, after the bell rang, Mouse angrily dropped the eye back in Lynn's pocket. "Okay for *you*, Lynn Morley!" she said. "It was all your fault!"

"Can't you take a joke?" Lynn asked.

"That's a joke? That's *sick*, Lynn! This is an eye. A dead woman's eye, and it's caused us a lot of trouble. I don't see anything funny about it, and I think you're acting pretty strange lately. That's the second time the librarian's bawled us out this week."

Lynn shook her head determinedly. "What's sick is letting the eye control us, or make us do things we shouldn't, as though we don't have any choice. A few weeks ago, Mouse, neither of us would have believed we could ever get to the point of rolling her eye down a library table. That means we're winning! It can't control us!"

"I don't know," Mouse said. She seemed to say that a lot lately. "But you're changing, Lynn. You might not realize it, but you're just a little bit different, and it scares me."

Lynn only laughed.

It was in bed that night that Lynn tried to remember a charm that she and Mouse had found once in *Spells and Potions*—a charm that was supposed to protect a person from witchcraft. She could only remember the very first word, which was "wind" and the last sentence, "Keep me safe from witches." Every time she opened her mouth, however, hoping that the right words would come, she heard herself whispering something entirely different: "Sing of morning, sing of noon . . ."

She frowned. She didn't even know she had remembered the words to the tune on Mrs. Tuggle's music box: *Sing of evening's silver moon* . . . She shook her head hard, but the words kept coming back: *Feel the darkness, touch the black, hear the shadows whisper back.*

Lynn turned over on her other side, feeling uneasy, not the reckless way she had felt the last few days. Was it so unusual, though, to remember something you had heard only once before—the tune Mrs. Tuggle had sung to her and Marjorie? She'd seen a pig's brain once, with lots of grooves in it, in science class. She wasn't sure, but she thought maybe all the little grooves were memories. Perhaps everything you ever learned made a path in your brain, so that if something triggered it off again, you *would* just naturally remember. Maybe it had nothing to do with witchcraft at all.

Lynn took the eye out of the pocket of her pajamas and turned over on her back, legs bent, balancing the eye on the top of her knees. When it rolled off, sliding down the sheet, she picked it up and tried again.

In the darkness, the eye seemed to glow. It twinkled, grew brighter still, then dimmed.

"I could crush you, you know," Lynn told the eye. "I could put you in a plastic bag, take you out on the sidewalk, and hit you with a hammer."

The eye winked again.

"Lynn?" came Judith's voice from the other side of the curtain. "Who are you talking to?"

"Myself."

"Come over and talk to me," Judith said.

Lynn slipped the eye back in her pajama pocket and padded over to the curtain dividing their bedroom. Judith rolled over and turned on her bed lamp. "Look," she said, and held out one arm.

"What?" Lynn said, trying to figure out what was different.

"Ken's ID bracelet!" Judith said proudly.

Lynn looked. There was a chunky-looking chain bracelet with a metal plate inscribed with KENNY on it.

"So why are *you* wearing it?" she asked.

"He gave it to me," Judith said dreamily.

"Why? It's his name, not yours."

"Oh, Lynn, you're so *dense!* That's the point! To let everyone know we're going together."

"Oh," said Lynn. She hated it when she didn't understand about dating. But *she* would never go around wearing a bracelet with someone else's name on it. If she was ever in an accident and unconscious, they'd think her name was Kenny. What a dumb thing to do.

"It's dumb," she said aloud.

Judith stopped admiring her bracelet and looked sharply at Lynn. "It is not!"

"It is! It's stupid! It's not even pretty. The metal's old, it's worn in places, and it looks cheap. I'll bet he got it at the five and dime."

Judith's eyes suddenly filled with tears. "Lynn! You just go back to your own side. I wouldn't have asked you over if I'd known you'd say that! You're just plain cruel!"

"It's the ugliest bracelet I ever saw," Lynn added. She was surprised herself. She didn't know why she kept on. One part of her wanted to apologize and the other part wanted her to say something even worse. She said something worse: "Only a jerk would give a girl a present like that."

Judith sprang up on her knees and struck out at Lynn. And just as suddenly, like a cat, Lynn struck back. The shock of fighting with Judith numbed her; as though watching a movie, she watched her own hands yank at Judith's hair. It had been years since they fought like this. Over and over they tumbled on the bed, kicking, scratching, clawing.

Suddenly the overhead light came on, and Mrs. Morley stood in the doorway.

"Girls! What on earth . . . ?"

Lynn tumbled off onto the floor and Judith leaned back against the headboard, a deep scratch

on one side of her face. It was a strange-looking
scratch, as though it had been made by an animal.

"I can't believe this!" Mother said, coming into
the room. "It sounded as though elephants were
clumping around up here." She stared at Judith's
face, then at Lynn. "You were *fighting!*"

Judith began to sob. "You should have heard
what she said, Mother! *Awful* things about Ken and
my bracelet." She grabbed a tissue and blew her
nose hard.

Mother focused on Lynn. "What's this all about?"

Lynn felt a rush of remorse. "I didn't really mean
it. It just came out that way."

"Well, did you girls have to fight over it? Isn't that
rather childish?"

"She started it," Lynn said lamely.

Judith was still crying. "I felt *so* good tonight.
And then Lynn had to ruin it all. It's like she gets
pleasure out of being mean."

"Judith, she can't ruin anything unless you let
her," Mother said. "If you like Kenny Phillips and
his bracelet, that's all that matters, isn't it? Come on
down to the bathroom and let me put something on
that scratch." She turned to Lynn then. "You should
be ashamed," she said, and went downstairs with
Judith.

Lynn *was* ashamed. She crept back to her own
bed and lay motionless, even after Judith returned,
sniffled some more, and finally turned out her light.
What *had* got into Lynn, anyway? It was perfectly
natural to *think* that Kenny's bracelet was ugly, and

that wearing it was stupid, but that was a lot different from saying so aloud to Judith.

She felt tears in her own eyes and remembered, suddenly, the way the girls used to make up after a quarrel when they were younger. The one who started it would go to the other and say simply, "Sorry." And then she'd add, "Friends again?" And if she was lucky, the other would say, "Okay." Even a "Maybe" would do.

So finally Lynn got up and went back over to Judith's side of the bedroom.

"Judith," she said softly, "I'm really sorry. Friends again?"

There was no answer.

"I just sometimes . . . well, I just act stupid, that's all. Friends?"

"I guess so," said Judith finally.

A flood of relief washed over Lynn. It felt so good making up. How could she ever have said what she did? What had made her *want* to hurt her sister? And how could she feel so differently about it now?

"Mom's right," Lynn went on. "If you like Kenny and want to wear his bracelet, that's what matters."

"You were just jealous, Lynn, that's all," said Judith.

Lynn swallowed. *Jealous!* Jealous of some dumb boy and his ugly bracelet? But even now she had no wish to hurt her sister, so she didn't even argue. "Maybe so," she said.

"Sit down," Judith invited, and Lynn made her way over to the edge of the bed in the dark and sat.

"Someday," Judith told her, "when you're as old

as I am, you'll have a boyfriend, too, Lynn, and it will be the best thing that ever happened to you."

Lynn tried not to gag. Judith was only three years older. She sounded like she was a grown woman of twenty.

"Someday," Judith went on dramatically, "you'll want a boy to kiss you more than anything else in the world."

Oh, gross! Lynn said to herself. She'd had to square dance once with a boy and his hands were all sweaty, and it was the worst experience of her life. If that same sweaty boy had tried to *kiss* her . . . ! But *still* she said nothing that would upset Judith.

"Maybe so," she said again, wondering how she could change so from one minute to another. "Well, sweet dreams, Judith," she added, getting up. "Dream of Kenny."

"I will. I dream of him every night," Judith told her.

As Lynn turned and started back toward her own side of the room, she suddenly felt the pocket of her pajama top and realized that the green glass eye was gone.

She stopped dead still in the middle of the floor, heart racing. It must have fallen out in the fight with Judith! Somewhere, on Judith's side of the bedroom, Mrs. Tuggle's eye was lying in wait, and Judith didn't even suspect. It might actually be in bed with her. *This* was why Lynn was feeling so generous now. This was why she no longer wanted to quarrel. The eye was somewhere else.

A wave of panic seized her. What would she do? She could hardly turn on the light and say, "Sorry, Judith, but have you seen a dead woman's eye around here anywhere?" She could hardly go rummaging about Judith's bedclothes, either, without telling her why. Yet there was no way she could go off and leave the eye there. Not with Judith unsuspecting. Not after what had happened last summer, when Judith came under the old woman's spell.

Lynn went over to her own bed, sat down on the mattress three or four times to make it sound as though she were settling down under the covers, and then, inch by inch, ever so slowly, she crawled on her hands and knees back to Judith's side once again.

Was it under the spread? On the floor? Behind the dresser? Should she wait until Judith had gone to sleep, then go downstairs and get a flashlight?

When she got past the curtain, however, Lynn noticed a faint green glow coming from beneath Judith's bed. She heard Judith roll over, and she waited. The green glass eye brightened, then dimmed. It winked again, and seemed to be beckoning.

Lynn heard Judith sigh and roll over. And finally, when Judith's breathing became deeper, more regular, as though she was on the verge of sleep, Lynn crawled forward a bit more, wedged her head and shoulders beneath the bed, and stretched out one arm as far as she could. And then, as her fingers circled the eye and pulled it out, the glow faded, but from somewhere, she didn't know where, an old woman's wavery voice began singing:

> *"Come, my nymphs, and you shall be,*
> *Silent images of me."*

chapter eleven

I'm afraid, Lynn wrote in her journal, *that I'm not myself when I'm carrying the eye. Mouse said I've changed, but except for what happened with Judith, I don't think so. I'm going to be more careful, though.*

On Saturday, she and Mouse went shopping. Strawberry preserves, Mouse had decided, weren't enough for her mother. When she visited her that summer, the first time she would be seeing her since Mrs. Beasley left the family last August, she wanted to take something more—something she'd have to spend a lot of money on to show how much she loved her.

"I don't get it," Lynn said as they went into the dollar store and checked the cosmetics counter for something that smelled good. "Why doesn't your *mother* spend a lot of money on *you* to show how much she loves you?"

"She doesn't have to," Mouse said. "I know she loves me no matter what."

Lynn didn't answer. A mother packs her things, moves out, leaving an eleven-year-old daughter behind, and the daughter knows she loves her no matter what? Then she thought of the past few months when Lynn's own mother had been under the spell of Mrs. Tuggle—when Mrs. Morley was grouchy and unkind, flying into fits of temper over small things. Lynn hadn't ever stopped believing in *her* mother's love, either. Sometimes things happen. Sometimes things make it hard for a parent to focus on anyone else but herself. Maybe it was as true for Mrs. Beasley as it had been for Lynn's mother, so Lynn kept her thoughts to herself. For a while, anyway.

They took the lids off all the containers of talcum powder and sniffed each one in turn.

"I'll bet she'd like lilac," Mouse said. "My brothers can remember when we had a lilac bush once, before I was born."

Lynn thought about Marjorie's two older brothers and how Mouse didn't get to see them often. There just wasn't much of a family left anymore.

"They can remember a house we lived in once with a huge tree and a swing in it too. All the good things happened before I was born, because when *I* came along, my brothers were in college and we were living in an apartment. I'll bet Mom thought she was all through raising kids. Then, *whammo!* Me!"

"So she got a nice surprise," Lynn said.

"I hope so," said Mouse. "They bought a house for me, anyway. That's when we moved here and Dad opened his bookstore. I wonder whatever went wrong between them."

"Whatever it was, it didn't have anything to do with you, Mouse."

"I hope not," Mouse said.

They went on past cosmetics, and Lynn followed Marjorie to the housewares section, and finally to lingerie. She was beginning to get a little bored with shopping and wished that Mouse would make up her mind. In the pocket of her jacket, she idly unwrapped the Kleenex from around Mrs. Tuggle's eye and rubbed it back and forth with her fingers, feeling its smoothness.

"Look, Lynn," Mouse called from up ahead. "This is what I was really thinking about for Mother. Do you think I should buy it for her?"

Lynn looked. Mouse was staring up at a mannequin in a red nylon nightgown. It reached to the floor and had thin spaghetti straps over the shoulders.

"That?" Lynn exclaimed. "It looks like an evening dress."

"I know!" Mouse said dreamily.

"Where would she ever wear it, Mouse, but to bed?"

"But it's only fourteen dollars! Mom always wanted to be a singer. I'll bet she could wear this as a nightclub gown and nobody would ever know the difference."

Lynn could hardly imagine Marjorie's gray-haired mother singing in a nightclub, much less in a red nightgown with spaghetti straps over the shoulders. She didn't know her nearly as well as Mouse knew Mrs. Morley, but Lynn still didn't think she would want a red gown.

"I'm not sure," she said finally. "How much do you have to spend, Mouse?"

"Six dollars and fifty-three cents. I could put the gown on layaway, and earn the rest by the time summer gets here."

Lynn knew it would take every penny Mouse got to pay for the red nightgown. Mouse didn't even know if her mother *had* a job singing. And even if she did, Mouse didn't know what kind of clothes her mother was supposed to wear. And even if Mrs. Beasley *was* singing in a nightclub, and *was* supposed to wear long dresses, Lynn felt quite sure that it wouldn't be the kind you paid fourteen dollars for in Woolworth's.

"Don't do it, Mouse," she said.

"Why *not?* I think it's perfect!"

"It's *not* perfect! You don't even know if your mom would wear it. You don't even know if it would fit."

"I can guess her size."

"Save your money. Just take her some strawberry jam like you'd planned, and then if she wants you to visit her again, you can start thinking about what to bring the next time."

Mouse stood very still and faced Lynn from across the lingerie counter. "What do you mean, *if* she wants me to visit her again?"

"Well . . . what I mean is . . . just see how you get along."

"She's my mom, Lynn."

"I *know* that, but she also walked out on you." As soon as Lynn said the words, she wished she hadn't. She saw Marjorie's lower lip begin to tremble.

"She d-didn't walk out on me. She just moved away."

"And didn't take you with her. One day she was here and the next she wasn't, and all you got was a note taped to the refrigerator," Lynn said hotly, angry at Mrs. Beasley and forgetting, entirely now, how it must sound to Marjorie's ears.

Suddenly Mouse turned and ran down the aisle toward the door.

"Mouse!" Lynn called after her, but Mouse went on. While customers stared, Lynn followed her friend outside. Marjorie was leaning against a telephone pole, crying.

"Mouse, listen, you've just got to face up to it!"

Mouse turned on her angrily. "What do *you* know about it? What do *you* really know about my mom and me? Were you there? Just because you want to be a psychiatrist, Lynn, you don't know everything about everybody. My mother loves me more than anyone could ever love *you!*"

Lynn walked home by herself and sat down on the porch. Two people in two days. She had managed to really hurt both Judith and Mouse by saying things she would never have said aloud, in quite that way, before. Instead of feeling guilty, however, she felt mad. Well, *let* them be angry at her. Sometimes you had to tell the truth. Sometimes you had to say what was on your mind, whether others liked it or not. Judith's ID bracelet *was* ugly. And Marjorie's mother *had* left with only a note to explain why. Was it Lynn's fault if Judith and Mouse couldn't face facts?

Stevie came bursting out the screen door, arms spread wide like an airplane, circled Lynn there on the steps, making a blubbering noise with his lips, then crash-dived beside her, bumping her arm.

"Knock it off," Lynn told him.

"Sourpuss," Stevie said.

It wasn't what Lynn needed to hear just then. She'd had enough for one day. "Stevie, stop it! Go find somewhere else to play. I just want to sit by myself."

"I can sit wherever I want," Stevie replied. "The porch belongs to the whole family."

"More me than you," Lynn retorted, without knowing why.

"Uh-*uh!*"

"Uh-*huh!* You're the tail end. We just picked you up along the way and added you to the family." Lynn meant it as a joke. Somehow she expected Stevie to giggle. Instead, he stared at her hard.

"You did not."

There was something about his trust, his hurt, his innocence, that made Lynn want to hurt him all the more. She couldn't explain it. "Yes, we did!" her voice went on. "We found you in a trash can."

"Lynn!" came Mr. Morley's voice from inside.

But Lynn didn't stop. It was as though her words were running away with her, as though her mouth were propelled by a motor all its own, and not even *she* could stop it. "We were walking downtown by the library one day when we saw these two feet sticking out of a garbage can, and there you were.

Somebody didn't want you, and had thrown you away."

Stevie started to cry.

The screen door banged open. Mr. Morley came striding across the porch, grabbed Lynn by one arm, yanked her to her feet, and swatted her hard, three times, across her bottom. Then he shook her.

"You've just been asking for it these past few days, haven't you? Any way you see to upset the family, Lynn, you do it. Well, this is enough! Understand?"

Lynn pulled away from him. "Yes." She ran inside and up to her room.

Her face burned with embarrassment. It had been years since her father spanked her. And there, in front of Stevie, he had spanked her as though she were still a little child. She was getting sick of this family!

For the rest of the day, Lynn kept to her room, working on the biography report (Amelia Earhart) for school, reorganizing her sock drawer, decorating her three-ring notebook, and putting a new pair of laces in her sneakers. She even took out the notebook she'd been using as a journal and wrote her thoughts about the absolutely stinking past two days as a member of the Morley family.

It was only later, when she was in the tub, soaking in a capful of bubblebath, that she began to feel more like herself and sorry for the way she'd been acting. It *was* an awful thing she had said to Mouse, but even worse what she'd told Stevie. How could she possibly have gotten any pleasure out of it? She felt no pleasure at all now in the remembering.

And then she saw the eye, the green glass eye, sitting on top of the toilet tank with her clothes, and she knew. When she had it in her pocket, she didn't *feel* evil, but she said some awful things. When she got away from it—in the bathtub, for example—she realized just how bad she had been. Maybe, when the eye was in her pocket, everything she did and said seemed perfectly reasonable, and it was only when the eye was somewhere else that she realized how unfair she had been.

Lynn sank down farther in the tub, letting the hot water caress her shoulders. Maybe she should try a scientific experiment: keep a journal of everything she did and said when the eye was in her pocket, and record everything she did and said when the eye was on her dresser instead.

Just in case it *did* affect her when it was so close to her skin, Lynn left it in her room when she went downstairs later to make a phone call.

"Mr. Beasley?" she said when Marjorie's father answered. "Could I talk with Mouse?"

There was a pause. "Well, you can talk to her, Lynn, but I'm not sure she'll answer back," he said good-naturedly. "I don't know what went on between you girls this afternoon, but Marjorie's been upset all day."

"I want to apologize," Lynn told him.

"Well, that certainly can't hurt. Hold on and I'll get her."

Mouse came to the phone. "Yes?" she said coldly.

"Mouse, I'm really, really sorry for what I said this afternoon. I've been making everybody miserable, not just you. Stevie . . . Judith . . . I think it's the eye."

"You can't go around saying whatever you want and then blame it on the eye," Mouse said. "I've got feelings, too, you know, and sometimes 'sorry' doesn't help."

"Of course you have feelings, Mouse! I've been hurting everybody. And the only time I feel bad about it is when I put the eye on the dresser and take a bath. When I'm away from it."

"Fine," said Mouse. "Then come to school on Monday naked and if you're nice to everybody, we'll know it was all the fault of a green glass eye."

"Seriously, Mouse. I want you to try an experiment with me."

"You want *me* to come to school without any clothes on and see what happens."

"I want you to carry the eye in *your* pocket for a day and I'll see if *you* act any differently."

"Oh, no," said Mouse. "No way. That's final!"

"Okay, then, pay close attention to *me* on Monday, because one day I'm going to leave it home and another day I'm going to have it on me, but you won't know which day is which. Just see if I'm any different. Okay?"

"I guess."

"Friends?"

"Maybe."

"Only maybe?"

"Sure, Lynn."

"And something else. Judith's going to spend next weekend with a girlfriend, so why don't you come and stay with me? We'll have the whole third floor to ourselves."

"O-*kay*!" Mouse said, coming to life.

Lynn hung up, relieved. That took care of Marjorie. Next she went upstairs to Stevie's room.

He was still awake, lying in bed with his lamp on, looking at his favorite bear book.

"Stevie?" Lynn said from the doorway.

"Go away, you old thing. You old stupid!" he said.

"I want to say I'm sorry, Stevie."

"You are not! You'll be mean again tomorrow."

"If I am, you can punch me right in the stomach," Lynn promised.

He looked at her warily. Lynn came over and sat in the rocker by his bed, the same rocker Mom used when she nursed him as a baby.

"I really was teasing about finding you in a trash can. I remember when Mom brought you home from the hospital, Stevie, right after you were born. You were so tiny that I could cover one of your feet with my hand."

Stevie went on turning the pages of his bear book.

"And sometimes, when Mom was feeding you, she'd stop and let me burp you. I'd put a towel over my shoulder and hold you against it. I'd sort of bounce you up and down, and after a while you'd give the *biggest, loudest* burp!"

Stevie giggled. "Like this?" he said, and faked a burp.

"Worse than that," said Lynn.

"Like *this*?" Stevie belched again.

"Yeah! Like that! And sometimes you'd spit up all over my shoulder."

"Good!" said Stevie, with satisfaction. Lynn reached over and hugged him, and Stevie hugged back.

For a long time Lynn toyed with the idea of going to sleep without the eye that night—of just letting it stay in a corner of her dresser drawer. She even got into bed without it. But her dreams were unsettling. Once she was sure she had heard something—or someone—knocking on the inside of her drawer. When she got up and turned on the light to check, the eye was still there, but it was not in the corner where she had left it, but on the other side completely. And once again, it winked.

Still, she shut it up again, going to bed without it, and later, heard the singing:

"Fast upon us, spirits all,
    Listen for our whispered call."

She got out of bed.

"Whistling kettle, tinkling bell,
    Weave your web and spin your spell."

Lynn took the eye out of the drawer, put it in the pocket of her pajamas, and climbed back into bed. It seemed to belong to her now, demanding to go wherever she went, do whatever she did. It seemed easier to give in than to fight it, and with the eye once more near her skin, Lynn promptly fell asleep.

chapter twelve

As far as Lynn could tell, the experiment worked, but what happened on Monday and Tuesday was so upsetting to both her and the whole family that it didn't much seem to matter.

"Five more days till the weekend," Mouse said on their way to school Monday. "What should I bring when I come to stay over?"

"Pajamas . . . toothbrush . . . the usual."

"Food?"

"Mouse, we've *got* food, for heaven's sake! We won't let you starve."

"You don't know how much I can eat."

"Yes, I do. If you want to bring anything, bring *Spells and Potions*. We could read it in bed."

"I've told you. I can't take it out of the store. And I especially can't bring it to your house."

They were walking to school slowly, arms around their notebooks. Mouse stole Lynn a sideways glance, and added, "But I've been reading a little on my own. Dad finally said I could read it as long as I keep it there in the shop."

"*Really?* What did you find out?"

"Right now I'm reading about how you're supposed to tell if a person is a witch or not."

"Well?" Lynn said impatiently.

"It's hard to tell. Witches don't go around with a big *W* on their sweatshirts, you know."

"But what did the book say?"

"The pages go on forever, Lynn, but it did say that a cake of feathers is a traditional sign of witchcraft."

"A *cake* of feathers? You mean like in 'eat'?"

"I don't know, Lynn. All it said was—"

"Or did it mean a bunch of feathers matted down like a cake of soap?"

"I don't know."

"Were the feathers on a person? In a person's house?"

"I don't *know*! I'm trying to tell you, Lynn. Sometimes you can read a whole paragraph of that book and still not know what it's talking about."

"Okay. What's another sign?"

"A cat or a rabbit that can talk. That's supposed to be a witch."

"Great. We'll go right out and look for a talking rabbit."

"Lynn, I'm *trying* to tell you what the book said."

"Okay. Sorry."

They walked a half block without saying anything at all. Then Mouse said aloud, "I wish we'd never met Mrs. Tuggle. I wish it had never happened."

"I wish that about a million times a day," Lynn told her. "What do you suppose we'd be talking about now if we hadn't?"

Marjorie thought it over. "Boys, maybe."

"Ugh! Not me! Not if I ever act as dopey as Judith.

Already she's wondering if she can stand to be away from Ken Phillips for one weekend."

Lynn did not let on that she was carrying Mrs. Tuggle's eye in her pocket and would leave it home on Tuesday. She planned to do the best she could, to act as though it weren't there—to think before she spoke, see if she could be kind and generous even with the eye in her pocket. So far it seemed to be working. She'd do the same tomorrow, leaving the eye at home. Then she'd ask Mouse which day was which. But that same afternoon, something happened.

At one-thirty, when the teacher announced that they could have the next half hour to finish writing their reports on the biographies they had read, Lynn, who had finished hers the night before, decided that it looked a little sloppy, that she could use the time copying it over to make it neat.

She sat at her desk, idly rubbing the glass eye, which was tied in a knot in the hem of her T-shirt, recopying "Amelia Earhart, Woman Aviator," with her other hand. At two, she handed it in with the others, and had gone back to her seat, waiting for the recess bell, when suddenly Mrs. Edmunds looked out over the class and asked, "Who's Dorolla?"

In the row next to her, Mouse turned her head slightly and stared, horrified, at Lynn.

Lynn felt her face growing warm. But it wasn't just her face. Her whole body felt flushed. It was like she felt sometimes when she had a fever—restless, irritable.

"Amelia Earhart," the teacher said again, impatiently. "Would whoever wrote this report please come up here and put your correct name on the paper?"

As though controlled by wires, Lynn felt her body rise from her chair, her legs move at the hips, bend at the knees. She bumped into other desks as she made her way down the aisle and then, as she snatched the paper rudely out of Mrs. Edmunds's hands, she heard a voice that didn't sound like hers at all, yet was hers: "My name *is* Dorolla." And she started back to her seat.

There were giggles from some of the class, stares from others, and Lynn could see Mouse, her eyes as wide as coat buttons, mouth open, face pale. Somewhere inside her head, Lynn knew that she should stop, turn around, and apologize. Somewhere in her head she tried to direct her feet to stop. And as she struggled with the part of her that had made her write "Dorolla," she felt sick, her legs felt shaky, and suddenly she bolted from the room and threw up in the hall.

The floor came up to meet her, the hallway went from light to gray to black, and when she opened her eyes again, she could smell iodine and antiseptic and vomit. Her mouth felt awful. She opened her eyes wider and saw a poster of an orange, a bowl of cereal, and a glass of milk, with the words "Three good ways to say good morning."

"Uhhhh," she moaned, and turned away. As she did, she looked right into the gray eyes of the school secretary.

"Feeling better?"

"A-a little. What happened?"

"Stomach upset, I think. Your pulse is fine. Let's check your temperature." She slipped a thermometer under Lynn's tongue. "I know. Your mouth feels yucky. As soon as I take your temperature, you can have a glass of water."

Lynn closed her eyes again and lay still on the health-room cot.

"This ever happen before? Throwing up and fainting?"

"Uh-uh."

"Well," the secretary said, taking the thermometer out and checking it, "Your temperature's normal. Try sitting up, Lynn, and tell me how you feel."

Lynn sat up. "Okay."

"Walk across the floor and let's see if you're wobbly."

Lynn obeyed.

"I tell you what. Stay here until school's out—fifteen more minutes—and then we'll have a friend walk you home."

Seconds after the bell rang at three, the door to the health room opened and Mouse peeked in. She came over to Lynn. "You okay?"

"Yeah. What happened?"

"You lost your cookies."

Lynn was embarrassed. "In front of the whole class?"

"No. Out in the hall. We could hear you, though, and two other girls got sick. Mrs. Edmunds called the janitor and he mopped it up. She and the principal carried you into the health room." Mouse stared at her some more. "Lynn," she whispered, "do you know what you *said*?"

Lynn closed her eyes a moment and nodded.

It wasn't until they were out of the schoolyard, on their way home, that Mouse said, "Lynn, you've got to get rid of that eye. It *is* the eye. You have it in your pocket today, don't you? It *is* making you do these things."

"Anything else besides writing 'Dorolla' on my report?"

"You're just not as nice as you used to be, Lynn, that's the truth. You've been acting strange in school, you sass the teacher, you even talked back to the *principal* the other day."

"But as long as I *know*, I can be extra careful."

"Maybe you don't have a choice."

"You mean someday I'll wake up and discover I'm Mrs. Tuggle?"

"All I mean is you can't go on like this."

Lynn stopped, and anger gnawed at her. "What do you want me to *do*, Mouse? Do you think I enjoy carrying it around? We tried hiding it, burying it. I don't dare ever leave it alone in my room. As long as I know where it is, then I'm still in charge. I think."

When they reached the Morleys' steps, however, they found Mother waiting at the door. "Lynn, you okay?"

"Sure. Why?"

"The school called and said you were on your

way home, that you'd been sick in class this afternoon."

"Yeah, it was really embarrassing. The room was
too warm, I think. But I'm fine now. In fact, I'm
starving."

Mother held open the door for them, but studied
Lynn closely as the girls came in. "Well, if you're
hungry, you can't be too sick, I guess. There are
brownies on the counter. Help yourself."

The rest of the afternoon went reasonably well.
After Marjorie went home, Lynn folded the laundry
for her mother and made a salad for their dinner.
Mother only mentioned Lynn's fainting in passing,
and nobody made a big deal of it.

It was after supper, when Lynn was brushing her
teeth, that they seemed to look brown to her. Old
teeth. Had she been forgetting to brush lately? She
put down the toothpaste and took out a can of tooth
powder, scouring her teeth well. Had that third
tooth from the middle always been that pointed?
Had she never noticed?

It was the following day, again after dinner, when
Mr. Morley called Lynn back to the kitchen after
the meal. Judith had gone to the library with Ken
Phillips and Stevie was watching television. When
Lynn entered the kitchen, her parents were still
seated at the table over coffee.

"Lynn," said her father. "Your mother got a
phone call today from the school, asking us to come
in tomorrow for a conference. Do you have any
idea what it's about?"

Lynn picked up a piece of leftover celery from a salad bowl and took a noisy bite, shaking her head.

"Not the slightest?"

"Probably about my fainting."

"And that's all?"

Lynn shrugged. "What did the *teacher* say?"

"The teacher said there has been a slight behavior problem. Anything going on at school lately that you haven't told us?"

For a brief moment Lynn's eyes met her father's. What kind of question was that? Of *course* there were things going on he didn't know about. Didn't *want* to know. Well, he did and he didn't. If she said no, she'd be lying. If she said yes, he'd tense up. What exactly was she supposed to do? She didn't answer.

"Lynn," Mother said. "Are you in some kind of trouble?"

"Not that I know of," Lynn said. "I hope not, anyway."

"Well, then, we'll all go to school tomorrow and find out," Father said. "I can get off work at three-fifteen, Sylvia. I'll meet you there."

Lynn was so upset the next day that she forgot her experiment and once again took the eye to school, as usual. "Mouse," she whispered, as soon as they took their seats. "You've got to do something for me. Dad and Mom are coming for a conference after school. I want you to keep the eye while we're in the principal's office so I won't do anything weird."

"What if *I* do something weird?"

"*Please,* Mouse! Just for fifteen minutes or so. I'll put it in a pencil box so you won't even have to touch it. Just sit on the bench around the corner from the office and wait for me, and I'll take the eye again the moment I come out."

"Lynn, I really don't like this—"

"I don't either."

"I wish we'd never heard of Mrs. Tuggle."

"Wishing doesn't help."

At a quarter past three, Lynn and her parents, Mrs. Edmunds and the principal, sat around a table in the principal's office over five cups of iced tea on the table before them. The principal smiled at the little group as she opened a packet of sugar, dropped it into her tea, and then sat stirring. Lynn's cup remained untouched.

"We all like Lynn very much," she said. "We've known both her and Judith since kindergarten, and now we have Stevie. When we enjoy a student as much as Lynn, we worry a little when we see a change in her."

Lynn, seated beside her father, wasn't even looking at him, yet she could sense the way his shoulders stiffened, the way his fingers tightened around his styrofoam cup.

"In what way has she changed?" he asked. Even his voice was tight. Very soft, very controlled, very matter-of-fact, keeping a lid on his feelings.

The principal turned to Lynn's teacher. "How would you describe it, Mrs. Edmunds?"

Lynn's teacher focused right on Lynn. There was

no beating around the bush where Mrs. Edmunds was concerned.

"Lynn seems unusually irritable lately. She snaps back at people as though her nerves are stretched just about as tight as they will go. Yesterday, as a prank, I guess, she wrote the wrong name on her report."

Mrs. Morley looked quizzically at the teacher. "What name did she write?"

"Dorolla," said the teacher.

Mother studied Lynn intently.

"And when I asked why she had used that name," the teacher continued, "Lynn marched to the front of the room, grabbed the paper from my hands, and said, 'My name *is* Dorolla.' It's really not like her at all. I'm mystified. But I'll admit that Lynn was simply not herself. It was just before she became ill that day, so perhaps that had something to do with it."

No one moved. No one spoke. And when the silence became too embarrassing to ignore, Lynn's father turned to her and said, "Well?"

Lynn stared down at her knees. She shrugged.

"Did you think that was funny, Lynn—writing the wrong name on your report?" the principal asked quietly.

Lynn shook her head.

"What made you so angry?" The principal just wouldn't stop. "Is that a name you always wanted?"

Lynn shook her head violently. "No!" she said, and her voice seemed loud in the small conference area of the room.

The principal folded her hands with the long, red-painted fingernails. "Sometimes," she said, as though choosing each word carefully from a platter, "things go on at home—even small things—that can make a pupil upset and anxious at school. I thought perhaps if we had a family conference, we might, together, figure out what could be going on in Lynn's life right now—either at home or with her friends or here at school—that is keeping her so on edge. If anyone has any ideas . . ."

Mother said nothing. Stared straight ahead. It was the name *Dorolla* that had upset her, Lynn thought. Perhaps, when Mother was under Mrs. Tuggle's spell, she, too, had been given a new name —a name that the old woman used to call out that part of Mother that was mean and uncaring. And perhaps Mother guessed that the name "Dorolla" had come from Mrs. Tuggle too.

Lynn was conscious of the silence in the room, and shifted uncomfortably in her seat.

"Sometimes," the principal went on, "we just can't seem to put a finger on anything at all. It's a puzzle to all of us. When this happens, it is often very helpful for the child to have a few sessions with a psychologist. We have an excellent one here in the county school system, a Dr. Long. Lynn, I think you would find it a comfort to talk to him a few times before school is over. He comes to our school on Tuesdays. Would that be all right with you," she asked, focusing on Mr. Morley again, "if we set up an appointment for Lynn?"

But Father was focusing on Mother. He did not

seem to hear the question, and when the principal asked it a second time, he said, "Of course. I'd appreciate it if you would. That okay with you, Lynn? I want what's best for you, honey."

It was like a string of dominoes, each person asking the other.

Lynn swallowed. It was not okay. Nothing would ever be okay again until she figured out what to do with the eye, how to keep it away from her family.

"Are we all through?" she said in answer. The others stared at her.

"We are, unless there's something you'd like to say yourself, Lynn," the principal said. "This is your chance to express your own feelings, surrounded by people who care about you. If there's any way at all we can help you, please tell us."

Lynn wanted, in the worst way, to say yes. She wanted desperately to say, "Here. Take the eye." She wanted to say that she wanted to go back to being Lynn Morley again, riding her bike through the streets and around the park, never thinking about witchcraft for the rest of her life. But she couldn't.

"There isn't anything you can do," Lynn said, and getting up, excused herself and bolted for the door. She rushed from the office and turned the corner, but the bench beneath the trophy case was empty. Mouse was gone.

chapter thirteen

"Mouse!"

Lynn stared at the bench where Marjorie had been sitting, then up and down the hall. The corridors were empty. There was the thunking sound of the janitor's mop hitting the sides of the wall in the all-purpose room as he cleaned the floor, but the only other noise was the sound of Lynn's own pulse, throbbing in her temples.

A moment later, she heard the low murmur of voices as her parents came out of the office with the principal, so she ran to the end of the hall and burst through the doors out onto the playground.

A boy was practicing shots over on the basketball court, but otherwise the schoolyard was empty. Lynn's heart thumped even harder. Maybe Marjorie had gone on home. She always had her mind on food when school was out, and perhaps the hunger pangs got too much for her. But again, maybe she didn't. Mouse had *promised* to wait until the conference was over, and sitting there on the bench, holding the pencil box with Mrs. Tuggle's eye inside it, she probably would not be thinking too much of food.

"Did you see a girl come out here?" Lynn called to the boy.

"I just got here," he said. "Didn't see anyone."

Lynn stood still in the center of the schoolyard and tried to concentrate. Slowly, like a glass ballerina on the lid of a music box, she turned in all directions, looking as far as she could see. And suddenly she caught a glimpse of Marjorie's orange-striped poncho off in the trees beyond the playground. Mouse seemed to be crouched low to the ground, and Lynn's heart beat wildly.

"Mouse!"

She bolted forward, her feet hitting hard as she left the asphalt and started across the field.

"Mouse!" she screamed again, and tore through the bushes.

Marjorie didn't even look up, and as Lynn slid to a stop in the soggy earth beside her, she heard her crying. Mouse had Lynn's pencil box in her hand, and was using it as a spade, gouging into the soft earth deeper and deeper, breathing through her mouth as she cried.

"Mouse?" Lynn asked more gently, trying to catch her breath. "What are you *doing*? Why didn't you wait?"

Mouse gave no answer, but continued her frantic digging. Her large owl-like glasses had slipped down her nose, and she wiped one arm across her face.

Lynn grabbed the hand holding the pencil box and stopped her. Mrs. Tuggle's eye rattled around inside.

"Mouse! Talk to me! What's the matter? Why didn't you wait?"

Mouse turned toward her, gulping back tears. "I'm burying the pencil box! I'm burying the eye, that's what."

"Why?"

"Lynn, I heard! I stood right outside the principal's office and I heard them tell your folks how you wrote the name Dorolla, and how they're going to send you to the school psychologist, and he'll tell your folks you're nuts, and they'll put you in a hospital or something. Lynn, we've got to get rid of this eye!"

"Listen." Lynn pulled Marjorie from a squatting position to a full seat on the ground and sat down beside her, one arm around her shoulder. "Just because you have one cavity doesn't mean you're going to lose all your teeth, does it? Just because you go to the doctor doesn't mean he's going to operate. Well, just because they're sending me to a psychologist doesn't mean I'm crazy. Don't talk dumb."

"But why *don't* we bury the eye, Lynn? It will be way out here in the trees, away from the playground, away from your house or mine, and we can forget about it."

"*Can* we, Mouse? What if the ground started sinking in and some little kid stepped in it? What if a dog dug it up and carried it into somebody's house? Remember what happened to Stevie when he found it in the ashes? It won't even burn! If I hadn't known what it was and figured it out, I don't know what would have happened to him—to us—to our family."

"Then what *are* we going to do?"

"I'm still thinking. But if I haven't got a better idea by next Tuesday, I'm going to turn it over to the school psychologist."

Mouse's lips fell open. *"What?"*

"Listen, Mouse. This might be the best thing that ever happened. If I'm ever going to be a psychiatrist, this will be wonderful training for me."

"But what are you going to tell him?"

"Everything."

"About Mrs. Tuggle and Judith? The crows? The cats?"

"Everything," Lynn said again. "The absolute truth. I'll reach in my pocket, pull out the eye, and give it to him. It will be his problem then. You *know* I can't give it to Dad. He'd just throw it out. He doesn't want to hear about all the things that are happening, because he's still worried about Mom. I could see it in his eyes today at the conference. I could see the way Mom acted when the teacher said the word 'Dorolla.' It must have stirred up some memory of Mrs. Tuggle's power over *her.*"

"But what will the psychologist do with the eye?"

"If he has any scientific curiosity, he'll do a study. Maybe he'll turn it over to a university for research or something. We don't have to figure out everything; we're just kids, Mouse. He's a grown man with training. And if they're sending me to a psychologist to talk, I'm going to talk."

"Whew!" Mouse began brushing the dirt off the end of the pencil box. "I feel a whole lot better already. I think I feel better than I have for a whole *year,* Lynn!"

"Good! I don't want you to worry about this any-more, Mouse. Let's think about this weekend. Judith's going over to her friend's right after school on Friday, then *you're* coming over, and we'll have two whole days together."

"Bring on Friday!" Mouse shouted.

"Bring on Friday!" Lynn bellowed even louder.

The boy with the basketball turned around far over on the court and stared in their direction. Lynn and Mouse burst out laughing. Lynn put the pencil box back in her jeans pocket and the girls went home.

The evening went so well that Lynn decided her parents weren't as upset as she'd thought they might be. Mother was quieter than usual, but not as quiet and distant as she'd been those first few weeks after the fire at Mrs. Tuggle's. Lynn helped her make a salad for supper, then folded the laundry, and she knew her parents were pleased that she was back to being a normal, helpful, cheerful person once again. It probably had to do with the eye still being in the pencil box in her dresser. For a little while tonight, anyway, she was going to keep the eye there just to make sure she treated her family kindly.

Then, as she was finishing her math problems, sprawled on her stomach on top of her bed, her father appeared in the doorway.

"Knock, knock," he said.

"Come on in. I was just finishing my math," she told him.

Mr. Morley sat down on Lynn's desk chair. Somehow he looked a little too formal. He must have felt it, too, because first he put one ankle over his knee, then put both feet on the floor again, and finally leaned forward as though trying to get comfortable.

"I'm just curious, Lynn," he said, smiling. "What made you write the wrong name on your report?"

"I don't know, Dad. I really don't."

He studied her. "No idea whatsoever?"

"I didn't even know I'd done it until the teacher said something. Maybe I'd been thinking about the name Dorolla and absentmindedly put it on my paper. Mrs. Edmunds got all upset about it, and it seemed so silly. Maybe that's why I told her that really *was* my name."

"That's just not like you, Lynn."

"I know. I can't figure it out either."

Lynn's father waited some more. "But why 'Dorolla'? Why not Betty or Susan or Charlotte? For some reason, it seems to have upset your mother."

"Do you *really* want to know, Dad?"

"Of course."

"You're not just saying that, and then, when I tell you, you'll get upset?"

"I can't promise I won't get upset. But I'm certainly not going to scold you or punish you, if that's what you mean."

Lynn took a deep breath. "Okay. When Mrs. Tuggle . . ." She stopped as she saw her father tense.

"Okay," he said, rubbing the back of his neck. "Go on."

"When Mrs. Tuggle was alive . . . that day Mouse and I were in her cellar . . . we protected ourselves by drawing a circle around us with a piece of Mrs. Tuggle's chalk."

Mr. Morley stared at her, unbelieving.

"You sure you want me to tell you this, Dad?"

"It's sounding more weird all the time, Lynn, but go on."

"We read somewhere that drawing a circle around you, with a witch's own chalk, can protect you from her power, and when we realized we were trapped in her cellar, Mouse drew the circle. Mrs. Tuggle was *furious*, Dad! She came rushing down the stairs, but she didn't try to cross the chalk line. Instead, she started calling us by our other names."

"Lynn, seriously now. What are you talking about?"

"She tried to get Mouse to come out of the circle by calling her 'Sevena,' and Mouse started to go. I tried to hold her back. Then she called me 'Dorolla' and it was like I was being pulled, Dad. Like I couldn't stop. Then you rang the doorbell, she went to answer, and we got away. You remember how we came rushing out, how scared we were. Well, that was why."

For almost a minute, they sat silently facing each other, not a word spoken. Then Lynn said, "Okay, I know. It sounds crazy. If I had a daughter who told me all this, I'd worry too. But it happened, Dad, just like I'm telling you. It was scary. It scares me now."

"It scares me too."

Lynn couldn't believe that her father had said that.

"It scares me that something like this . . . whatever it is . . . could get such a hold on my family."

"It's witchcraft, Dad."

"We don't know that. But it is certainly something strange that I don't understand. I'm glad you're going to be talking with the school psychologist, Lynn. I'm just too close to this, too worried, to see it rationally. I'll feel a whole lot better if someone outside our family listens to what you have to say. In the meantime, don't use that name—Dorolla—in front of your mother. Okay? It frightens her."

"You don't have to worry. I don't want to have anything to do with that name. I hate it. I wish I'd never met Mrs. Tuggle. I wish she'd never come. I wish I could spend the time thinking about summer and picnics and swimming and stuff, instead of . . ."

She almost said "the eye." Did she dare tell him? Was this the time? She sat quietly a moment or two. If she *did* tell him, and showed him the eye, and told him what had gone on in Stevie's room the night she found it, she felt quite certain that he would take it away from her, that he would throw it in the trash or something, and would not believe all the things the eye had done. No, she had better wait.

"Instead of what, Lynn?"

"Worrying about all of you. Whether or not we'll be okay. Whether we can ever really escape Mrs. Tuggle."

"Well, sweetheart, we're certainly going to try. Now. Marjorie is coming for the weekend, isn't she?

That's something to look forward to. And starting next Tuesday, you can sort things out with Dr. Long, and I'll bet that by summer we'll be the same old Morleys again—going on trips, eating ice cream, having fun." He came over and gave her a bear hug, then went downstairs.

Lynn swallowed and blinked back tears. She loved her dad. Loved all of them. With all her heart, she wanted to be eating ice cream and riding her bike and not worrying the way she was now.

It was an uneasy feeling, having the eye next to her again as Lynn stuck it, wrapped in three layers of Kleenex, into her pajama pocket and climbed into bed. She was more tired than she had thought. It had been a rough day.

Sometime during the night, however, she heard someone calling. It was an old voice, a quavery voice: "Do-*roll*-a! Do-*roll*-a!"

"Shut up," said Lynn.

"Do-*roll*-a, come . . . !"

Something brushed Lynn's forehead, she was sure of it. Sleepily, she stretched out one hand and pawed the air in front of her. Nothing was there. For a moment she thought she heard a flutter. She rolled over on her back and listened some more. But she was just too weary, and when she opened her eyes again, it was morning. The sun streamed through the window on her side of the bedroom, and Lynn felt sure that she had only been dreaming. The eye was still in her pocket and she herself felt fine.

But she could not explain what happened on Friday. The English assignment had been to write a mood poem. Without naming the mood, the students were to portray, by the words they chose, what the mood was, and the other students were to guess. One boy did a poem about a clown, and he used words like "rollicking," "smiling," "bouncing," "skipping," and of course the class guessed "happy."

Mouse had made up a poem about getting up in the morning and kicking a chair and banging silverware on the table, and the class guessed "grumpy."

Lynn stared at the words on her own paper when she stood up to read her poem. She could not believe she had written what she did.

"Lynn?" the teacher said, waiting.

Helplessly, Lynn propelled herself to the front of the room:

> "Sing of morning, sing of noon.
> Sing of evening's silver moon.
> Feel the darkness, touch the black,
> Hear the shadows whisper back."

The class sat absolutely still when she had finished.

"What a lovely poem, Lynn!" Mrs. Edmunds said. "What do you think, class? Does anyone have an idea about the mood she's describing?"

"Sleepiness?" someone guessed.

The teacher looked at Lynn. Lynn shook her head, eyes on her feet.

"Happiness?" asked someone else.

"No," Lynn said miserably, in almost a whisper. She dared not look at Mouse.

There were more guesses, none of them right.

"I guess you'll have to tell us," said Mrs. Edmunds. "What kind of feelings did you have when you wrote the poem, Lynn?"

"F-fear," Lynn said hesitantly, and quickly took her seat.

"Well, even though we didn't guess your mood, it's a good poem," the teacher said. "The last line especially, and I can well see how those words might bring about a spooky feeling."

Lynn remembered getting the assignment, remembered sitting down at home to compose a poem, but she did not remember writing this one down. She knew it wasn't hers. Yet there was Mrs. Tuggle's music-box poem, in her own handwriting, there on the paper.

When school was out, she went up to the teacher.

"That wasn't my poem," she said.

Mrs. Edmunds looked at her curiously. "Whose poem was it, Lynn?"

"I don't know. I heard someone sing it once. There's a tune to it on a music box. I didn't think I'd written it down. I didn't—" She swallowed. "I didn't even know I still knew the words."

The teacher was puzzled. "I'm glad you told me the truth, Lynn—that you used someone else's poem. And you know, I think you're going to feel a lot better next week when you have a chance to talk with Dr. Long. We've already set up an appointment for you. He's a man who really listens."

Lynn found Mouse waiting for her when she went outside.

"I couldn't *believe* it, Lynn! I couldn't *believe* you'd read that poem in class."

Lynn was miserable. "Me either. Maybe I *do* need a psychologist, Mouse. I didn't even know what was on the paper till she called my name." They started down the sidewalk toward home, but Lynn was conscious of Mouse keeping to the far side of the walk instead of walking next to her as she usually did, their arms bumping casually together.

"Mouse, don't *you* be mad at me. I didn't do it on purpose. I went up and told Mrs. Edmunds it wasn't my poem."

Mouse continued walking, eyes straight ahead. "It's not just that."

"Well, what is it, then?"

Mouse glanced at her, then turned away again. "I don't know, Lynn. You just seem different. You . . . even *look* different somehow. Even your voice is different, just a little."

Lynn stopped. "How? How do I look and sound?"

"Older."

"*How* old?"

"*Old* old."

"You think I'm becoming Mrs. Tuggle." They were the most frightening words Lynn had ever said aloud—the most frightening thought she'd ever had. The moment she said them, she realized it was a fear that had been gnawing at her ever since she started carrying the eye around. The eye. The awful eye.

"I'm still me," she insisted. "When you come over tonight, Mouse, things will be like they always were."

Mouse didn't answer.

"They *will,* Mouse! Dad and I had a talk last night. I told him everything except about the eye. And for the first time, I think he believed me. He said he was scared, too, and was worried about me. Just knowing that it's his problem, too, not just ours, makes me feel better."

That seemed to make Mouse feel better too. "Well, why didn't you *tell* me that? If just one other person—a grown-up person—believes us, Lynn, maybe he'll do something." She gave a sigh. "Whew! I feel *so* much better. I'm hungry. I'm starved! Can I come for dinner? Dad's making macaroni. What are you having?"

"Tacos, I think. Dad's driving Judith over to her girlfriend's, and I'll help Mom make dinner. Come around six."

Despite the poem Lynn had read in class, she did feel much better when she reached home—glad that she had told Mrs. Edmunds the truth about the poem, glad she had told her father about Dorolla, glad she had told Mouse that she'd told her father and Mrs. Edmunds, glad that she didn't have to worry all by herself. Even though she still carried the eye in the pocket of her jeans so that Stevie could not possibly get it again, she felt more herself that evening than she had in a long time. She helped her mother make tacos, played a game with

Stevie, had the table all set by the time Mouse came over and her dad got back.

"Well, I just get rid of one daughter and I get another," Mr. Morley said jovially, smiling at Mouse as he sat down at the table. The dinner hour was merry, with Dad making jokes and Mom teasing Stevie about his "milk mustache," and Lynn and Mouse devouring three tacos each, topping off the meal with butterscotch sundaes.

Nothing happened that night. The girls practiced headstands in the third-floor bedroom, painted each other's toenails with Judith's nail polish, tried on some of Judith's shirts, and then played cards till after midnight. There were no strange sounds, no singing—a normal night in the Morley house— Lynn sleeping in her own bed, Mouse in Judith's.

Once Lynn got up in the night to go to the bathroom, and just for an instant, when she looked in the mirror, she thought she saw someone behind her—an old woman in a hood. But when she whirled around to look, she discovered only Mother's blue bathrobe hanging on a hook on the back of the door.

Saturday morning the girls slept late, ate breakfast on the porch, and read comic books in the sun that came through the screen. By the middle of the afternoon, however, the sky began to darken, storm clouds moved in, and when Stevie got home from his swimming lesson at the Y, it was already beginning to rain.

"We're going to need raincoats tonight, Richard," Mother said as she dried Stevie off.

"Where are they going?" Mouse asked Lynn as they lay on their backs on the rug and tried to read, holding their books above them.

"To a movie with friends."

"We may go back to the Swansons' after the movie and make pizza," Mother called from the hallway, "so don't worry, Lynn, if we're not back by midnight. It may be one or later, but their number's by the phone."

"We'll be okay," Lynn said, and then to Mouse, "we already laid in a supply of cocoa, marshmallows, peanut butter, and bananas."

"Chocolate grahams?"

"We've got those too."

Lynn thought she was feeling just fine. She had spent a perfectly normal day with Mouse. But somehow, as she watched the headlights of her father's car backing down the drive, she felt fear again—completely unexpected. She was home, she was warm, she was loved, but still . . .

The poem she had read in class came back to haunt her:

Feel the darkness, touch the black,
Hear the shadows whisper back.

chapter fourteen

"Let's make popcorn!" yelled Stevie as soon as the car was out of sight.

"Hey, we've got to have dinner first," Lynn told him. "Cheeseburgers okay?"

They sat around the kitchen table, listening to the steady drumming of rain on the window glass.

"Does your dad get lonesome when you're over here?" Lynn asked Mouse, slipping a carrot stick on Stevie's plate when he wasn't looking.

"I think so. I spent all day with him at the bookstore, though, to make up for it."

Lynn let Stevie stay up longer than usual. She didn't know if she was getting sick or what, but she felt restless, almost feverish. Afraid that Mouse might notice and decide she shouldn't stay, Lynn focused on Stevie after they had made popcorn, reading him five different story books, including *The Five Chinese Brothers,* his favorite, while Mouse hammed it up, silently acting out the characters' parts and making both Lynn and Stevie laugh. When it was Stevie's bedtime at last, he went without argument, and seemed glad to have his head upon a pillow.

Upstairs on the third floor, Mouse enjoyed walking around Judith's side of the big bedroom, unscrewing the caps on her cologne bottles and sniffing each one. "It's like a palace up here," she said. "I'm the queen and you're the king. Did you ever see the way kings and queens eat, at opposite ends of a long table with seventeen candles in the middle? When they want to talk to each other they have to shout."

"I'll bet that's not the way it really is," Lynn said. "I'll bet they eat breakfast in their pajamas just like everyone else."

The rain seemed louder there on the third floor. It beat against the shingles and pecked at the window glass. When the wind gusted, it whistled through the cracks around the windows, a high, piercing whine.

After they had both taken baths and put on their pajamas, Mouse glanced warily at the bulge in Lynn's pajama-top pocket. "How do you ever *sleep* with that thing, Lynn?"

"I manage. I'm afraid of what might happen if I don't."

"I'd be afraid of what might happen if I *did*."

They lay on their backs on Judith's bed with the bowl of leftover popcorn.

"The way I see it, Mouse, the worst thing that could happen would be for the eye to get lost or stolen or something, and we didn't know where it was. We wouldn't know if it was close by or far away, whether it was affecting us or not. It's scary to keep it on me, but scarier when it's somewhere else."

Mouse was tossing popcorn in the air, piece by

piece, trying to catch it in her mouth. "I was reading some more of *Spells and Potions* at the bookstore this morning," she said after a bit.

"What did you find out? *Tell* me!"

"Not much. But it did say that witches hate the color red, they don't like anything made of coral, and I think I have a new charm we can use."

"You do? What is it?"

"Do you have any horseshoes?"

"No. Why would we have horseshoes? We don't have any horses."

"Well, you're supposed to nail three horseshoes to your bedpost—"

"We don't even have a bedpost."

"—and then you say these words." Mouse reached over to where her jeans were lying and pulled a slip of paper from one pocket:

> "Suns that sear and fires that roast,
> Nail all evil to this post.
> Thrice I smite with stone or rock,
> With this mell I thrice do knock.
> One for Bod,
> And one for Wod,
> And one for Lok."

Lynn turned her head and stared. "What's that supposed to mean?"

"How do I know? You said to look for charms and I found one so I copied it down."

Lynn snatched the paper from her. "What's 'mell'?"

"I don't know."

"What's 'Bod' and 'Wod' and 'Lok'?"

"Search me."

"Oh, for Pete's sake, Mouse, how is this going to help? All you do is nail three horseshoes to your bedpost and say these words and witches can't hurt you?"

"It didn't say anything about witches. It protects you from marsh-fever."

Lynn sat up. "Oh, Mouse, you're so *stupid*!" she yelled in exasperation. "We're not in danger from marsh-fever, we're in danger from witchcraft. I'm trying like everything to keep my family safe and you safe and everybody safe, and all you can come up with is a charm for marsh-fever. You're *dumb*!"

Mouse started to bawl, and this seemed to annoy Lynn even more.

"Oh, stop it! Stupid charms and stupid tears, and I'm the one who's doing all the worrying."

Mouse jumped up and reached for her jeans. "I'm going home."

This time Lynn's voice softened. "Oh, Mouse, I'm sorry. Really! There I go again, shooting off my mouth. I'm just plain scared and I take it out on everybody. I'm really sorry."

Mouse glared at her and plunked back down. "I'd like to see *you* sit down with *Spells and Potions* for a whole afternoon and try to make sense of it. Most of those charms were for things I never even heard of. The only other one I found is the one we already know."

"Which one is that?"

"Where you take a ring of someone who has died, wrap it in silk, bury it under an oak tree for one night, dip it in vinegar, and hold it over the flame of a candle while you recite three times: 'Wind and water, earth and sky, keep me safe from witches.' And after that you have to wear it constantly, because if you take it off for even a minute the power is gone."

"Did we try that?"

"Don't you remember? I took the ring my grandmother gave me before she died, and we did all that, except it fell off once when I was playing the piano and I never went through it all again."

Lynn settled back against the headboard, thinking. "What if we took Mrs. Tuggle's eye, wrapped it in silk, buried it under an oak tree, dipped it in vinegar, and held it over a flame? Do you think that would take all its power away?"

"Where's the nearest oak tree?"

"Down the street."

"So who's going to go out in all this rain to bury the eye? And what if it washes away in the night?"

Lynn sighed and thought some more. She almost volunteered. Her legs ached with restlessness. A walk—even a walk in the rain—might help. She still felt somewhat feverish. Rain might help that too. But she said, "What if we did only part of it? Part of it would probably be better than nothing. We could do everything except bury it."

"Oh, Lordy, Lynn, I don't know . . ."

"We've got to show the eye we're not afraid of it. Judith's got a silk scarf. We'll wrap it in that for a while, then we'll go downstairs, dip it in vinegar, hold it over a flame, and say the charm."

Mouse crept quickly under the covers, pulled them up to her chin, and watched while Lynn took a scarf from Judith's dresser, Mrs. Tuggle's eye from her pocket, and wrapped the blue scarf around the green glass eye.

They left it there while they took turns reading *The Midnight Fox* to each other. Then they checked the eye. Nothing had happened. The rain outside was coming down a little harder and the wind was stronger, but the eye merely winked and looked the same as it had before.

"Okay," said Lynn. "Let's dip it in vinegar."

"Lynn, we're really asking for t-trouble," Mouse said, peering over the top of the bedspread. "How do you know that when we use the eye we're not becoming a *part* of the witchcraft instead of trying to keep it away?"

"Because we're using the witchcraft protection charm, that's why. We're not calling on devils and demons, Mouse. We're trying to get the heck away from them!"

Mouse gave a deep sigh. "Okay," she said, and climbed out of bed.

Lynn started downstairs to the kitchen, Mouse behind her, the blanket wrapped around her shoulders and trailing on the stairs.

"M-maybe we should check Stevie and make sure he's okay," Mouse said. "We're going to wake him going up and down the stairs."

"Not Stevie," said Lynn. "He sleeps like a log.

Once, after I'd been sick and Mom had given me dinner in bed, I was carrying a whole tray of dishes back to the kitchen and dropped it right outside his door. Stevie didn't even wake up."

But she peeped into her brother's room to make sure. The little boy was sound asleep, breathing peacefully beneath his Donald Duck night light there on the wall. Lynn went back out and closed the door.

Down in the kitchen, she poured a cup half full of vinegar.

"What do you want to happen, Lynn? The eye to dissolve or what?" Mouse asked, watching from a distance.

"I'll take whatever we can get," Lynn said. "Even if this only gives us *half* protection from witchcraft, I'll take it." She dropped the eye in the cup, and as it sank into the vinegar, it gave off a strange hissing sound, like a snake.

Lynn jumped backward. Mouse tripped over the blanket, trying to get out of the way. They clutched each other as they cowered against the wall. A foul-smelling mist seemed to rise from the cup, but slowly the hissing stopped. Outside, the rain came down harder still. Lynn could hear it gurgling down the gutters, hitting against the pane.

When Lynn's breathing returned to normal, she crept forward and peered into the cup. The eye seemed to glisten and glow in the vinegar, giving it a strange green cast.

"W-what time will your folks be home?" Marjorie asked.

"Late. The movie isn't over until eleven, and then they're going to some friends' house. Not before one, I guess."

Since nothing else seemed to be happening with the eye, the girls got out a package of chocolate grahams and some milk. At twenty after eleven, the phone rang. Lynn bolted for the hall.

It was Mr. Morley. "Lynn, we just got to the Swansons' house in all this rain, and we wondered how things are going there. No leaks in the roof, I hope."

Lynn knew that her father was not worried about leaks in the roof. He was worried about her. "I don't hear any drips," she answered.

"Good." There was a pause. "Everything okay? Stevie in bed?"

"We just checked, Dad. He's sound asleep."

"Great. Well, we left our number by the phone, sweetheart. Call us if you need to—any reason at all."

"We will."

There was another pause. "Your mother wants to be sure all the doors are locked."

"Yeah, they are, Dad." Lynn wished that her father would stop asking questions. The more he asked, the more uneasy she became.

"Well, Main Avenue was under a foot of water near Spring Street, and I just wanted to be sure the house wasn't floating away. I think that your mother and Marie are getting ready to make a pizza, so don't worry if we're not home before two."

"Okay. Have a good time."

There was something about knowing she could reach her parents, something about having the Swansons' number by the phone, that made Lynn feel better when she hung up. Brave, even. She went back into the kitchen and checked the eye. It continued its greenish glow.

"Okay," she said. "Time for the chant. You hold this match, Mouse. I'll put the eye in a spoon and hold it over the flame. We'll both say the words."

She gave Mouse a long kitchen match, and after the flame glowed brightly, then settled down to a yellow light, Lynn put the eye in a teaspoon, held it over the flame, and the girls said the words together:

> "Wind and water, earth and sky,
> Keep me safe from witches."

Nothing happened until they said the word "witches." Then suddenly the flame flared up in a burst of fire, making the spoon too hot to hold, and Lynn dropped it. The eye rolled across the kitchen floor and came to rest against one leg of the refrigerator, winking . . . winking. . . .

"Oh, Lordy!" Mouse collapsed into a chair, clutching the blanket tightly around her. But Lynn began to smile.

"You know what we're going to do next, Mouse? Boil it."

Mouse scooted away from the table, away from Lynn. "Boil the eye?"

"Boil the eye."

Lynn got a saucepan, filled it with water, and put it on the stove.

"Lynn, don't!"

Lynn just laughed. "Boil and bubble, toil and trouble—"

"*Please*, Lynn!"

Again Lynn was conscious that she didn't feel very well. Her lips seemed changed or something, the skin around her mouth tight. She turned the flame up high.

For almost three minutes, Mouse said nothing. Sat in the corner watching Lynn. When the water was bubbling hard, Lynn walked across the floor, picked up the eye, and then, holding it above the pot of boiling water, dropped it in.

Instantly there was a flash of lightning outside the window, followed immediately by a loud thunderclap.

Mouse leaped off the chair and bolted out into the hallway.

"Take it out, Lynn!" she pleaded. "Take it out!"

Lynn hesitated, but a moment later the lightning came again, and the thunder seemed almost instantaneous. Lynn grabbed a pair of kitchen tongs, thrust them into the water, pulled out the eye, and turned the fire off. When the eye had cooled, she put it back in her pocket.

"Don't do that again, Lynn. Don't do anything more with the eye," Mouse begged. Then, "You're really acting weird, Lynn. You *look* weird."

"How?" But even as she said it, Lynn realized that her voice sounded strange even to her.

"I don't know. You've got wrinkles around your mouth."

Lynn raised one finger and felt around her lips. "They're chapped, that's all."

"Let's go upstairs and wait for your folks. Okay?" Mouse started for the stairs. "Okay?"

Mouse led the way, and Lynn followed. She stopped in the bathroom, however, and when she looked in the mirror, Lynn decided that she *did* look strange. There *were* little wrinkles around her lips, the way she looked sometimes in winter, when her skin was very dry and chapped. She smeared some lotion around her mouth.

When they reached the bedroom, Mouse said, "I don't want to sleep alone, Lynn. Stay over here with me, at least till your folks get back."

Lynn agreed. She didn't particularly want to be alone on her side of the bedroom either, not in a storm like this. She was thinking about the lightning that had struck Mrs. Tuggle's home, burning it to the ground. If lightning struck the Morley home, she told herself, she would rush downstairs with Mouse, grab Stevie, and get him outside. She rehearsed it in her mind and that made her feel better.

She lay for a long time, listening to the rain throbbing on the roof. But she didn't feel sleepy. Her legs had that jumpy, restless feeling again, wanting to walk, to run. She tossed from one side to the other.

"Boy, I can see why you and Judith don't sleep in

the same bed," Mouse said after a while. "Sleeping with you is like sleeping with a windmill, Lynn."

"I've got the jumps," Lynn told her.

They were quiet for a little longer, and then Mouse asked, "If the eye had its way, Lynn, what do you think would happen? What does *she* want to happen?"

"What do you suppose, Mouse? She wants to get rid of us. Get rid of us or get us to join her coven, like she always wanted."

"She hasn't got a coven, Lynn. She's not even here."

"She's got a witches' coven," Lynn said darkly. "Wherever she is or *what*ever she is, she's trying to build up a cone of power again, trying to get a group of people under her power, just as she tried with Judith and Mother and us. It never stops. It just never seems to stop."

"Maybe boiling her eye did more good than we thought."

"We'll soon know, I suppose," said Lynn. "I wish it was one o'clock. I wish Dad and Mom were home."

Downstairs, the clock chimed midnight.

Mouse settled down under the blanket. "I think I'm ready to go to sleep," she murmured.

"I'm not. Do you ever get restless legs?"

"Uh-uh."

"Restless arms?"

"Good night, Lynn."

"Restless head?"

"Go to sleep, Lynn."

For at least a half hour, Lynn tried her best to lie quietly, and when she absolutely had to turn over, she did it as slowly and quietly as possible, making the entire turn in slow motion, inch by inch.

This is ridiculous, she thought. *Maybe I ought to go over in my own bed so I won't wake Mouse up.*

She was just about to get up when she heard a faint noise: *the fluttering.* It seemed to start at the far end of the room, coming closer and closer. At one point it seemed so near to her that Lynn was sure she could reach out and touch it. Her eyes popped wide open and she stared up into the darkness. Almost at once the fluttering began to recede until there was no sound left but the drumming of rain on the roof.

Was it the bat again, Lynn wondered, if it was a bat at all? The same bat that had come into the bedroom the night her father removed the storm windows? She had not heard it for some time, and assumed it had gone out the same way it had come in. Lynn pulled the blanket up over her head, wondering what to do next.

Minutes passed, and then the noise came again, closer still, flying directly past Lynn's ear, scraping against the sheet.

"Mouse!" she said, shaking her friend.

Mouse slumbered on.

What should she do? It seemed selfish to wake her up. Perhaps what Lynn should do was to get up, open the bedroom door, and turn the light on in the hall. Then she could get back in bed, watch, and as soon as she saw the bat fly through the doorway, attracted by the light, she could hurry and close the door again and let her father deal with the bat when he got home. Stevie's door was closed, so it wouldn't bother him.

Slowly Lynn lowered the sheet from her head, thrust one foot out from under the blanket, searching for the floor. Just as she sat up, however, as though it had been lying in wait for her, the noise—the fluttering—came straight at her. This time as it passed, sharp points scratched her cheek, like fingernails, and Lynn screamed.

Mouse sat up like a shot. "What's the matter?"

"S-something's in the room! I think it's a bat."

"Oh, Lordy!"

Before Lynn could stop her, Mouse rolled over, turned on Judith's bedside lamp, and then they saw it—a huge bat, wings spread, coming right at them.

chapter fifteen

The girls screamed and dived under the covers.
Again the creature scratched at the sheet as it
passed, the fluttering directly over their ears.

When it stopped circling and the noise quieted,
Lynn tried to catch her breath. She could hear the
thump, thump of her own heart.

"L-Lynn, I never saw a b-bat that big," Mouse
whispered.

"Neither did I. It looks horrible! I'm sure it's a
bat, though. Listen. Slowly reach out your arm and
turn off the lamp. Then I'll get out of bed, go turn
on the hall light, and we'll wait for it to fly out.
Then we'll close the door."

"I'm too scared."

"It's the only way, Mouse."

Slowly Lynn uncovered her head and looked
around. At first she couldn't see it. Then she spotted
it on the wall just above Judith's window. It had a
long snout, long pointed teeth, and even a long
tongue, which it flicked occasionally to one side.
There was a growth on its nose that resembled a
horseshoe. Mouse finally uncovered her head to
look, then quickly covered herself again in terror.

"We c-can't just open the window and get it out of
the house?" she whimpered.

"Dad put the screens on last week." Lynn cautiously put one leg over the side of the bed again, eyes on the bat. But Mouse grabbed her.

"Lynn, I hear singing!"

Lynn listened. Now that one foot was on the floor, however, she didn't want to stop. She felt almost desperate to move, to jump, to run. Anything. The strange thing was, *she* couldn't hear the singing.

"What's the song?"

"*You* know! It's that 'Come, my nymphs,' song. Don't go, Lynn!"

Lynn couldn't understand it. She heard nothing at all except the squeak of springs as she put the other foot on the floor.

Mouse suddenly let go of her arm. "*You're* singing it, Lynn!" She scooted away from her in terror. "*You're* singing that song!"

And then Lynn realized that her lips were moving —her dry, wrinkled lips were forming the words as though she had been humming it to herself all along. At that moment, she heard something else: "Do-*roll*-a!"

"Oh, L-Lordy!" Mouse gasped.

Lynn got slowly out of bed.

"*No*, Lynn!"

"Do-*roll*-a!" the call came again. And it was then that Lynn realized it came from the bat.

As though leading the way, the bat flew to the door of Lynn's room, waiting for her to open it. And trancelike, her dry lips still singing the song, Lynn followed and opened the door.

Suddenly Mouse was on her feet, too, pulling the blanket off the bed, rolling it up in her hand like a sack, and then lunging across the room, swinging the blanket, trying to hit the bat.

The creature circled, swooping low around Mouse's face, wings fluttering menacingly, its beady eyes intent on Lynn.

"Hit it, Lynn!" Mouse cried. "Hit it!"

But Lynn, opening the bedroom door, felt as though her legs belonged to someone else. She moved out into the hallway and started downstairs. She sensed her lips still singing, sensed the bat directly overhead now, then flying on ahead of her, leading the way.

"Lynn!" Mouse screamed from the top of the stairs. "Where are you going? Open the back door and maybe it will go out."

Lynn didn't answer. She wanted to tell Mouse that she would. Wanted to say she'd turn on the back porchlight, open the door, and wait until the creature was gone. But even as these thoughts swirled through her mind, she knew she was going outside with the bat. Knew that her feet would take her there.

"Do-*roll*-a!" the bat called, hovering overhead. And then the words, "Come, my pretty!"

Lynn walked across the kitchen floor in her bare feet and unlatched the door. She stepped out on the screened porch, its floor wet with blowing rain, and unlocked the second door. Rain pummeled against her. The bat flew out and Lynn followed. Down the wet steps and across the soaking grass toward the garden.

She could hear Marjorie calling from the back door. She could feel the wind, the wet, the water—the squish of mud between her toes as her bare feet reached the garden. Against the black of the sky, she could still make out the huge bat, just overhead, circling, waiting for her, leading her on. Once it swooped low and seemed to cackle like an old woman in her ear: "Dorolla, my nymph, my sweet, my pretty."

Weakly Lynn raised one arm to push it away. Her fingers felt stiff, and as she rubbed them together to warm them, they did not feel like her fingers at all —bent and dry and wrinkled with age. Terrified, she ran a finger over her lips. Instead of the smooth skin she was used to feeling, she found deep ridges and furrows. She was no longer herself! She was old! She was . . .

Marjorie's footsteps sounded behind her now, and the closer Mouse came, the more furiously the wind blew, the harder Lynn was pelted with rain. Already her pajamas were plastered against her body like tissue paper.

"Do-*roll*-a!" the voice crooned. "*That's* my pretty! Only a little farther now. Come down to the water, dearie! Come, Dorolla, come!"

As Lynn left the garden and started across the field she could feel her feet sinking ankle deep in mud. Already she could hear the roar of water in Cowden's Creek as it overflowed its banks.

She could not tell where Mouse was because the

wind was howling so, and drowned out every sound but the persistent calling: "Come, Dorolla— to the water, dearie!"

Lynn made a conscious effort to stop, but she could not even feel her legs now, as though her whole body was numb. She seemed to have nothing but ears that were working—listening to the call and obeying.

She thought she heard Mouse somewhere behind her, but her eyes tried to focus on the water ahead. In the blackness of the night she could just make out the handrails of the little footbridge that crossed the creek. The floor of the bridge itself was underwater. Lynn could not tell where she was supposed to cross and then she knew that she was not to cross at all, but to go on into the water.

"Do-*roll*-a!" the voice came still again.

"M-Mouse! Help me!" Lynn managed to cry as she started down into the creek—the water up to her calves, then her knees, her thighs. "It's the eye! Grab the eye!"

There was a splash behind her, and then she felt a hand on her arm. At the same time, a powerful gust of wind almost knocked her over, but the hand held her up. The hand became two hands, then two arms.

"Give it to me, Lynn! Give me the eye!" Mouse was saying.

But Lynn could not. She felt very weak, very old. Her legs seemed to buckle as the water swirled around her, and she leaned against her friend. She felt Mouse's hand searching her pajama top, her pocket. Then fingers inside the pocket. Finally, as she struggled against the current, Mouse's arm around her, Lynn saw, through the darkness, Mouse draw back her arm and fling the eye as hard as she could out into the churning water.

For a moment both girls continued to stand in the creek, holding on to each other, the rain hitting at them, the wind howling, and above the roar of the water there came a hideous screech—part bird, part bat, part woman, part witch.

Instantly both girls turned, leaped out of the water, slogged back across the muddy field, then the garden, then the yard, hair and eyelashes matted with water, pajamas drenched and clinging to their bodies.

Stevie was standing in the doorway, crying. "Where *were* you?" he sobbed. "Lynn, I was scared!"

Afraid to let him see what she had become, Lynn knelt down quickly and put his head against her shoulder, turning her face away. But she caught a glimpse of her hands as she held him, and they were her own hands once again—not stiff, not old, not wrinkled. Slowly she raised a finger to her face. The skin around her lips was smooth and moist.

She swallowed, then swallowed again, almost afraid of her own voice. "There was a bat in the house, Stevie, and we were trying to get it out." Even as she said the words, she knew how ridiculous it sounded, kneeling here in her drenched clothes, but it was reason enough for Stevie.

"I called and you didn't come. I heard all the noise and woke up and you were gone!"

"I'm sorry we woke you," Lynn said. "Mom and Dad will be home soon. Everything's okay, Stevie. We got wet, but we chased the bat outside, so we can all go back to sleep now."

She dried him off, gave him a kiss, and Stevie trotted upstairs again. Lynn glanced toward the clock. Almost one. But it was another moment before she could look at Mouse.

Marjorie stood by the door in a puddle of water, pajamas clinging to her bony knees, mud between her toes.

"M-Mouse," Lynn said weakly, "you saved me, you know."

"I know," Mouse said.

"If you hadn't caught up with me, I—"

"Don't say it, Lynn."

"You must have been *terrified*. The way I was acting, the way the wind was blowing, the water, the bat. But you came after me anyway!"

"I *had* to, Lynn. I just had to."

Lynn got a towel from the kitchen drawer and another for Mouse. As they dried themselves, Mouse said, "You were singing her song, Lynn. You were . . . you were even beginning to look like her."

"She would have drowned me if you hadn't come. But you *did* come, Mouse. You're stronger than you know."

There was no singing now. No one calling. The bat had gone out into the night from which it came.

When the kitchen was clean, the floor mopped, and the door locked once again, the girls went back upstairs for fresh pajamas, but they did not go to bed. They sat at the window overlooking the garden, the field, the creek, sharing a blanket around their shoulders.

Somewhere the green glass eye was rushing and rolling down the waters of Cowden's Creek toward the Wabash River. From there it would reach the Ohio, then the Mississippi, and finally, Lynn hoped, the sea.

ABOUT THE AUTHOR

PHYLLIS REYNOLDS NAYLOR has loved scary books and stories since she was a young child. To be truly frightening, a book should have as its setting ordinary people in a familiar place, she believes, and this is why she enjoys writing the Witch books, featuring Lynn, Mouse, and their adversary, Mrs. Tuggle.

The author of more than sixty books, including *Witch's Sister, Witch Water,* and *The Witch Herself,* as well as *Night Cry, The Agony of Alice,* and *Alice in Rapture, Sort Of,* Phyllis Reynolds Naylor has received, among other honors, the Golden Kite Award from the Society of Children's Book Writers, the Child Study Award from Bank Street College, the annual book award from the Society of School Librarians International, and the Christopher Award. She has won the Edgar Allan Poe Award from the Mystery Writers of America and was awarded a grant from the National Endowment for the Arts.

The author and her husband live in Bethesda, Maryland, and are the parents of two grown sons, Jeff and Michael.

ABOUT THE ARTIST

JOE BURLESON attended Art Center College of Design in Pasadena and lives in New Jersey.